MW00763251

THE SWITCHED

G.D. SACCO

Galaxy Books
New York, New York

First edition published 1999.

All characters contained within this book are fictional. Any similarities of name or other likeness to actual individuals are coincidental.

Cover design by Foster & Foster. Characters illustrated by Chris Harris. (As shown: clockwise- Nathan, Emily, Franky, Troy)

The Library of Congress has catalogued this edition as follows:

Sacco, G.D.
    The Switched / G.D. Sacco. --
  1st ed.
    p.cm.
    LCCN: 99-61910
    ISBN: 0-9671358-9-3

    1. Alien abduction--Fiction. 2. Unidentified flying objects--Fiction. I. Title.

PS3569.A223S95 1999   [Fic]
            QBI99-548

ATTENTION ORGANIZATIONS, HEALING CENTERS, AND SCHOOLS OF SPIRITUAL DEVELOPMENT:
Quantity discounts are available on bulk purchases of this book for educational purposes or fund raising. For information, contact Galaxy Books, 244 Madison Avenue, PMB 231, New York, NY 10016 or call (877) GALAXYB / fax (212) 428-6747.

To my loving wife, Susan.
Quite literally, it could not have
been done without you.

✳ ✳ ✳

To all those who remain in silence.

✳ ✳ ✳

And to Emily. I kept my promise.
Your turn . . .

Contents

ACKNOWLEDGMENTS

I would like to thank all those who inspired me to write this book. Which include some of those listed below, however, listing everyone would have taken too many pages.

Special thanks to Susan Sacco, Brenda and Frank Sacco, Linda and Tom Price, Kathy and Tom Sacco, Frank Sacco Jr., Robin and Robert Solitare, Daniel Pure, Dr. Frederick Ringwald, Professor Darden Pyron, Carl Sagan, Ian Stewart, Dr. David M. Jacobs, Stanton T. Friedman, John E. Mack, George Foster, Chris Harris, and Jacques Vallee.

FROM THE AUTHOR TO
THE READER

"Many, perhaps most, and maybe even all mature stars may have planetary systems. This is an encouragement to aspiring interstellar space travelers."

-Carl Sagan
"Pale Blue Dot"

Today, with all of our sophisticated and advanced technologies, including the Hubble Space Telescope, and the radio telescopes in Puerto Rico and New Mexico, we can see the very edge of the known universe. Our galaxy, the Milky Way, contains an estimated 400 billion stars. Most of these same stars are like our own medium sized star, the sun. Many of those same 400 billion stars have planets orbiting, like in our own solar system.

Yet, our Milky Way galaxy is only one of another 80 billion galaxies! Each of those 80 billion galaxies have hundreds of billions of stars, and thus trillions of planets. Although these numbers are staggering to imagine, they describe the enormity of our known universe. How could anyone, for one second suggest, that the hundreds of trillions of planets within our universe contain no life - that those trillions of planets are either barren icy rocks, or boiling globes, circling stars across a lifeless expanse of space? How could anyone assume that this planet Earth, full of wonderful and diverse life, be the exception in the universe? Mathematically, THERE MUST BE OTHER LIFE OUT THERE!

At the same time, reports of strange objects in the sky

continue to roll into police stations, and Air Force bases across the globe. People of all races, across all national boarders are seeing and reporting the same things. This has become known as the U.F.O. phenomenon. There are countless detailed reports that people have even been abducted by strange non-terrestrial creatures, taken aboard their U.F.O. and given a physical examination. In some cases, these abductees have lapses in their memory, where they can not remember where they have been over a given period of time, only later to discover that they were abducted.

Usually, the abductee first learns of his or her pervious abduction after undergoing hypnosis. Many researchers in the U.F.O. field have begun to share notes on their studies, including results of individual hypnosis cases. I have included some quotes at the start of selected chapters from such researchers.

Still, the debate rages on. Ufologist, as they have become to be known, say that the U.S. Government is covering up what it knows about the alien presence on Earth. The government refutes these claims and insist there is nothing hiding in the Pentagon files regarding U.F.O. activity. Most of the argument stems from a July 2, 1947 Roswell, New Mexico incident. That night something crashed in a farmer's field. The following day, the Roswell Air Force base released to the press that they had recovered a "flying disk." Within 24 hours, the Air Force retracted that statement, announcing that they really recovered a downed weather balloon. Of course, ufologist have a hard time buying that for 24 hours the Air Force mistakenly identified a downed weather balloon for an extraterrestrial vehicle.

Major Jesse Marcel, who was the first on the scene in Roswell, told the press in 1978 that the Air Force pressured him into keeping silent about what was really recovered in the desert that night in 1947. Marcel told the media that the Air Force had in fact recovered a U.F.O. He said he was forced into a massive conspiracy to hide the truth about the crashed "flying disk."

Many other witnesses of the Roswell incident have since come forth in support of the late Marcel's claims. Many of the dozens of witnesses not only saw debris from the "flying disk," but claim to actually have seen dead alien bodies. These same witnesses apparently have nothing to gain by saying such things. Some have even claimed that they were threatened by men dressed in military uniforms . They say that they were told not to repeat what they saw. While many did repeat their accounts, it was only within close family circles. That is until Marcel came forth with his story. So, what is the truth?

Why would the U.S. Government want to hide the truth about extraterrestrial visitors? Some speculate that in the forties and fifties, the government feared that if the public thought that aliens were abducting their children at night, there would be a crazed public panic. Indeed, if the public was told that information today, there would be little argument against the idea that a widespread panic would ensue. Others, meanwhile, suggest there has been some sort of deal struck between the major world governments and aliens from afar. Whatever the case, the U.F.O. phenomena continues to create controversy among those willing to listen to some of the mounting evidence that is being amassed by the ufologist.

In the fall of 1997, a workshop was convened at the Pocantico Conference Center in Tarrytown, New York, in which a group of conservative, and diverse professors, scientists, and investigators formed a scientific review panel in an effort to look at the UFO issue in a purely scientific manner. Those on the panel came from around the world, and from leading universities, including Stanford. The panel reviewed only physical evidence, ". . . with clear recognition of the dangers of relying wholly on the testimony of witnesses." The panel concluded that further study of this phenomena should be done. And that some physical evidence was being withheld by various military organizations.

If for nothing else, the importance of the Stanford Science Panel of 1997, shows a growing acceptance of the UFO phenomena to mainstream science. Only under the conservative investigation of such scientists, will we see the hard evidence necessary to find the truth.

In my view, to refuse to at least examine that evidence, whether because the entire notion *seems* absurd or not, is a cultural throw back to the days when fear of knowledge and uncertainty retarded humanity's progress until the enlightenment period. The idea of extraterrestrial life in itself is not bold. In fact, you'd be hard pressed to find an astronomer or physicist who believed life was limited to planet Earth. The real question is whether that life is technologically advanced enough to allow passage to our world.

One factor, astronomers are quick to point out is, that our galaxy is relatively young compared to other nearby galaxies. This difference in galactic ages could allow extraterrestrial species a million or so years of maturity over humanity.

In any case, any species advanced enough to travel light years to get to Earth, must be both ethically and evolutionarily mature. One thing everyone agrees upon is that such a species could easily overpower and dominate the human race, if they so chose. What *they* want, *they* will get.

So, supposing that another civilization has found Earth in the distant corner of the Milky Way, and that there is an interest is us, what do *they* want? To *them*, humans would most certainly appear primitive. As primitive as we to *them*, as neanderthal to us. Thus, if aggression was a factor, it'd already be long over for humans. "GAME OVER" would've been flashing years ago. *They* must be here to study, or help.

This account of an alien abduction of a ten year old boy exposes the human frailties in us all. Relatively speaking, humans are the new kids on the block that is called planet Earth. With that in mind, certain comparisons can be drawn between young Franky Carter and the infancy of humanity. In the book, young Franky becomes the embedment of humanity, as he discovers how far his species has to go before truly becoming civilized. We, as a civilization and species, are still learning who we are, where we are, and how to get what we want. Indeed, we have only begun to crawl. *THE SWITCHED*, is an examination of human nature, where in the end, we are shown how to stand up, walk, and then run.

Readers can contact the author by writing to:

Gary Sacco
PO Box 9
Grenloch, New Jersey 08032

"I shall never believe that God plays dice with the world."

-Albert Einstein

Chapter One

Outlander

"I am often asked how I would react if the entire abduction phenomenon should prove to be the internally generated product of people's imaginations - if there are in reality no abductions and no aliens, and never have been. If that were true, I would weep with joy. I want to be wrong."

-David M. Jacobs, PH.D.
"Secret Life"

September 16, 1965
11:15 p.m.

The rain fell harder than either of them had ever seen before. Each clap of thunder shook the 27 year old mother of three as she trembled in the parked Plymouth Belvedere. Her soaked husband, Thomas, rushed to finish changing the flat tire, as the car sat on the shoulder of the dark deserted hillside road.

"Hurry up!" she pleaded through the closed window. "I told the babysitter we'd be home an hour ago."

Thomas could only manage a nasty glance. But something in that glance caught his eye. Through the reflection in the window, a bright beam of moonlight broke out across the glass, glaring out his wife's spellbound face. "The moon? On a stormy night?" Thomas wondered.

His wife's frantic window pounding snapped him out of his trance as he spun around. Before either could react, they had become engulfed in a radiant white light, many times brighter than the sun.

Oddly, neither Thomas or his wife would remember the brilliant light that night. Nor would Thomas remember fixing the flat tire. He'd only remember driving home half asleep, and dazed. And when they finally arrived home at half past three in the morning, they woke the babysitter without explaining the lateness. Nine months later, Thomas' wife gave birth to a baby boy, Frank.

October 15, 1976
2:00 a.m.

The grandfather clock in the suburban New Jersey home's living room struck two, and as the stars outside began to dance, ten year old Frank, slept soundly. One star fell suddenly and lit up a farmer's field 100 yards behind his home.

As light invaded the blinds of the bedroom window, he opened up his eyes and stiffened his back momentarily, like something was tugging on his legs. Frank relaxed and sat up out of bed as if in a trance. Quietly, he made his way through the dark house until he reached a large wooden door that led to a basement and back door. White light pierced through the door frame and poked its way through the key hole, as his trembling hand reached to turn the dead bolt and unlock the door. Without control of his actions, Frank turned the lock, allowing the door to swing open and permitting the white light to engulf his body. A dark skeleton-like shadow, cast on the opposite wall, glided up the stairs toward him. . .

For the first time, Frank opened his eyes. As he lifted his head off a bare wooden table, the intense sunlight filled his squinting face. Frank looked around the forest clearing and found himself surrounded by hundreds of people. Though he did not recognize anyone, nearly everyone appeared to be about his own age, and as his eyes adjusted to the sunlight, he could tell that everyone else seemed to be just as disoriented as he. Some appeared asleep, while others frantically looked around for a familiar face, only to find others doing the same. Slowly, a soft chatter arose.

Naturally, Frank's first thought was, "Where am I?"

A boy sitting behind him at another table, as if reading

Frank's mind, said, "We're just off the coast of Fathom Sound. We're not there yet, but it feels like it, doesn't it?"

"Yeah, except . . ." Frank stopped himself from finishing. "No! Uh, where are we?"

"I just told you, didn't I?" replied the boy now looking away from Frank.

With that Frank questioned his state of reality. He nervously deducted that he must be still dreaming. He closed his eyes tight and counted to five, then slowly peaked open his right eye, hoping to see his bedroom ceiling. No such luck.

Frank noticed an adult man walking nearby. "Hey mister, where are we?" he yelled.

The man smiled slightly and pointed toward one end of the massive field. Frank stood up on top of the table to get a better look. His jaw dropped when he found himself at the center of thousands of children.

Just then the sound of a microphone came crackling from the direction the man had pointed. All of the children immediately quieted as they looked off to that direction. A women standing on one of the far tables finished adjusting the microphone to her height. "Good morning. My name is Elizabeth. I'm sure all of your are wondering what's going on. Well, let me just ask a question, how many here have ever been to a summer camp?"

Some in the crowd raised their hands prompting everyone to look about for a estimated inventory to the question. "Good. Well, this is just like camp, only better. And for those who have never been to a summer camp, you're going to have the best time of your lives these next couple of days. And in a few days, you'll be back home, and back to school." Of course, even mentioning the word 'school', forced moans from the audience. "Someone will be with each of you soon to answer any questions you have."

Then, almost on cue, the ground began to shake. The trees swayed to life, blowing side to side, as a deep roar rose from behind a bank of trees. The roar grew louder and filled the air that seemed to now shake.

Frank turned, as did the crowd, toward the sound. Many clapped as dozens of large green transport helicopters passed over the unusual trees lining the field. They passed overhead and began landing on an adjacent field.

Frank's heart pounded in his throat as he still stood on top of the table. Dazed, he didn't immediately realize that someone had gently grabbed his hand. "It's okay," someone said as she softly tugged on his arm to lead him down off the table. "You will be okay, everything will be all right."

Frank stepped down off the table as the woman introduced herself as Emily. Emily was tall for a women measuring just over 5' 9". She kept her blonde hair pulled back into a short pony tail, which accented her athletic build. Looking up at her, Frank had three questions, as she lead him across the field toward the awaiting helicopters - Where was he? Where was he going? And when was going home? The growing loud rush of the helicopter blades didn't permit posing any of those questions at the moment, but he set a promise to himself that he was going to get some real answers soon, or he was going to become very uncooperative.

Frank noticed a circular logo on the helicopter's side as they boarded. It had two dots, one on the left and one on the right side of the circle, and two arch shaped arrows each pointing to different dots. Then he remembered the man in the field that he spoke to earlier had the same symbol on the back of his shirt.

The helicopter rose, and they cleared the trees.   Frank

sat by the sliding door and was therefore able to see partially into the cockpit. He noticed two pilots up front, and through their windscreen, he could see they were heading toward open ocean. Ahead, he could see a cloud. As the craft approached it, it appeared to be square. They passed by it, and he stood up to get a better look as it streaked by. It was definitely square. Perfectly so. And there were others, also perfectly square, all spaced evenly apart. With that he sat back down. Curiosity turned to apprehension. "I've never seen clouds like that before," he thought. Yet, for a reason he could not yet explain, something felt very familiar about everything he saw. The circular symbol, the clouds, the odd trees, and even Emily. So much so, he somehow knew to refer to her simply as 'Em.'

The trip ended with a purposeful panoramic aerial of an island that Frank knew was Fathom Sound. About the size of Hawaii, Fathom Sound looked like a tropical oasis with postcard beaches, and massive mountain peaks. The two peaks rose to heights above the freeze level, allowing snow to crest the peaks, which on this day created a halo of fog.

The helicopters landed on the beach front. Together these green machines unloading on the beach, reminded Frank of an old war movie he saw on television. He laughed deep inside. "This is not war," he thought. Somehow he now understood that this was a place he agreed to come. Why or how he came to that understanding, like everything else, he was not sure. Whatever it was, this had a powerful calming effect of Frank at a time when panic could easily overcome a ten year old's sense of reason.

He stepped out of the helicopter and onto the beach. There were about forty children on Frank's helicopter so they stayed together in a group as they were led off the beach. Each child had an adult with them. Frank noticed that each adult had the same symbol on the back of their shirts.

They followed a winding trail through the heavy vegetation. Frank looked up at Emily and asked, "Where are we going?"

"This path leads to a small village. That is where you will be staying these next couple of days. Come on, I'll show you where you will be sleeping," she said with a hop in her walk.

They came up over a ridge on the outskirts of the village. Most of the groups had broken off and gone down separate trails by the time Emily reached Frank's sleeping shack. Frank looked around the sloping shaded village of shacks. "Not much of a village," he thought.

The shacks were snug with only a bed, a table, and two chairs. They also appeared identical from the outside. There was one window on each side of the shacks. A simple dark green fabric was used as shades. The walls were made of old warped planks. The entire ceiling could be propped up like a sun roof. This provided lighting during the day. Candles were used at night.

Frank sat on the bed, "Okay Em, lay it all out for me. I mean, I know I've been here, and seen those square clouds before, but refresh my memory, where are we?" he said almost matter of fact.

Emily drew a smile. "You're going to do just wonderfully here. Your intuition is fooling your mind though. Everything feels familiar to you, but you don't remember anything or anyone. The reason is very complicated, and unfortunately my answer may not be what you had in mind," she said growing more serious. She crossed the room and opened the window by rolling up the green fabric.

"We're in a special place," she said as she sat on one of the chairs. "To you, 'square clouds' makes this place magical. To me, I see square clouds and think, hmmm, that one cloud's corner is not so perfect, I wonder what could be wrong? You see Frank, the people here are in such perfect harmony with nature, that nature itself has changed. It has become ordered. Perfect. Symmetric. So when I see a cloud that is a little odd shaped, I worry."

"You can call me Franky. That's what my friends and family call me. Will we be taking the helicopters home too? Um, I mean, how far is home?"

Emily's eyebrows rose as she calmly moved her chair closer to Franky. "That's the really hard part to believe, Franky. It's a long story. You see, you're a very special kid. And I need your help. In fact, so does everyone you know back home. Do your remember those dreams you've been having lately? About the white skinny creature that takes you out of your bed at night?"

"Yeah! But how. . ." he said wide eyed as Emily cut him off.

"They were not dreams," she said flatly. "Franky, I know you can't remember everything, but during one of those times at night last week, you were asked if you would like to come here to Fathom Sound. And, well, you said that you would. So, here you are."

Franky looked confused, and a little more anxious as he remembered how scared those dreams made him. "But, where's Fathom Sound?" he said slowly. "That's like Hawaii, right?"

"Not quite," Emily said with a crooked smile. "Look Franky, I'm going to be straight forward with you, you're not on Earth anymore. You're over 65 million light years away from Earth right now."

Franky sat back on the bed stunned. "But how. . . I mean, then how do I know you? Are you someone I know at home?" he asked after collecting his nervous thoughts.

"No, we have never met."

The fact that Franky was somehow off the surface of Earth was just now hitting him as he sat in shock. "Earth?" he screamed. "Earth! What do you mean we're not on Earth? What are you, some kind of Martian?" he said as he scurried away from Emily to the other side of the bed.

"No! No, of course not, Franky. I am just as human as you. And there are no aliens here on Fathom Sound, not right now anyway. And as long as things go right, you won't see one for the five days of your visit," she said trying to ease his natural fear of the creature from his nightmares.

"But, you will learn about them, and from that, you will learn to understand the world around you. How nature works and reacts to the people in it. Though you will remember none of this, you will carry the lessons home with you, and they will remain inside you forever," she said leaning back. "I said that you were special. You are. You see, right now, you are much smarter than you were back home. A boy of your age might find some of the topics we are going to learn about too complex to understand. So your ability to learn has been altered while here on Fathom Sound. Also, your current basic understanding of nature is more advanced."

"So, when I go home, I'm going to forget ever being here? And forget everything I learn?" he said confused.

"Basically, yes. But, only temporarily will you forget the lessons learned at Fathom Sound. As you grow into a man, several years from now, and your mind in trained at high school or college, some of the lessons learned here, will begin to trickle back to you. You see, you can't understand concepts without fundamental background knowledge. So, as you learn those fundamentals through your education at home and in school, those lessons learned at Fathom Sound will emerge. The lessons will emerge inconspicuously, and may appear to you as if you have come up with original concepts about the way nature works. Many details will never be remembered. And you will not remember this island or anyone on it, including me."

Emily paused for a moment, "You will be here for only five days. By the way, each day here is only twenty-three and half hours. Your absence will not be noticed at home, nor will you notice any lapse of time after you get back. During your time here starting tomorrow, you will learn about people in society, and how they react with nature. Now, I told you earlier that I needed your help, and here's why . . . those creatures, or aliens, they are friends. They are on a mission to help people learn how to be in harmony with nature. Once this is accomplished, amazing things will begin to occur on Earth," Emily said with a wonderful smile.

"Like square clouds, right!?"

"Well, I wouldn't call that amazing. But I guess you could say that's along the same lines that I'm talking about," Emily said as she stood and gazed out the window. "You see, everyone in this village was brought here, by their own choice, to learn. The aliens have been doing these five day lessons with people from Earth for thousands of years. And slowly, over that time, these lessons are starting to make a difference. After you and the rest of this group here on Fathom Sound go home, and the lessons emerge, you may decide to change the way you interact with nature. And if enough people do the same, well . . ."

"I know, I know . . . square clouds!" he said smiling.

"Yes, but that is only the beginning. The aliens call it, Devout Reality. It's what the alien's ancient ancestors called, the unity of nature and consciousness. Many people from Earth say it is the unity of science and religion. All of that will be taught to you over the next few days, and then you will be sent back. This should be a fun experience for both you and me."

"Is there a giant classroom on Fathom Sound?" Franky asked after he realized the only structures he saw were the individual shacks.

"No. Each student has his or her personal teacher. I will be your very own teacher."

The sun had now set. Emily lit a candle using ordinary wood matches. "I'm sure you're not going to be able to sleep at all without knowing my involvement here and more about the aliens, right?" Emily said sensing Franky was still very uneasy, despite the island's calming influences.

It was a question on Franky's mind at the moment. Emily seemed to take the words right out of his head. Franky nodded.

"I am involved here only because it's what I wish. I love it here. I am a volunteer. I train boys and girls from Earth in Devout Reality. I work one on one with the aliens in between groups of children from Earth. I also work and live with the other resident instructors. When not on Fathom Sound, the instructors and myself live in a city called Atlantis."

"So, you're like an alien?" Frank asked with hesitation in his voice.

"No. I'm human. Just like you."

"Don't you ever go home, I mean, back to Earth? Don't

you have a family?"

"Nope, I think of the other instructors here as my only family, and Atlantis as my only home. And unlike nearly all of the other instructors, I was once on Earth, but I can never go back. I made a decision a long time ago that gave me a one way ticket. But I have no regrets. I truly love my life here."

"My situation is unique," she continued. "I'm one of the few instructors here that was actually born on Earth. I was once a student, just like you. I liked it here so much that I left Earth, but that was a very unusual event. Many students at first are frightened, or homesick, in the beginning, but more often than not, they want to stay longer at the end of the week. Franky, you have no choice, I want to make that clear. It is very easy to fall in love with this island, but you must return home on time, you must understand that from the beginning."

"Oh, you won't have a problem with me. Trust me! But don't you miss your mom or dad? How could you just leave for good?"

Emily grew somber, "That's a long story . . . but, for you, I'll tell it. You see, my mother died when I was very young. And my father, well, he was very mean to me."

"You mean, he'd like hit you?" Franky asked uncomfortably.

"He was a very bad man, and that's all you need to know about him. Anyway, when I came here, my instructor Nathan, he convinced the aliens to let me stay on as a resident/student instructor. And so, here I am."

"Didn't anyone miss you?"

"I don't know, I never looked back," she said trying to hold back her emotions.

"Well, how is it that no one's going to notice that I'm

gone for five days?" Franky asked.

"This is one thing you're going to have to trust me on, for now. It'll be clear how when you return home. All I can say now is that you will be returned home to your bed on the same night you left - which was last night."

"About the aliens, where do they live?" he asked.

"Not on this planet. Not on any planet. That's something that's really hard to explain without you knowing how Devout Reality works. Ask me again in five days. Right now, I will tell you this about the aliens. There are nearly a hundred trillion of the species that brought you here. That's an unimaginably large number of any species. That means, for every person back on Earth, there is over 20,000 aliens! But, they no longer reproduce. They also no longer age. They have stopped the aging process genetically. They survey the galaxies, looking for intelligent life, life that can be taught peace, that can be taught Devout Reality. But they do this in a manner that will not directly interfere with any civilization's natural social evolution. So they seek out young children looking for healthy boys and girls. But first, each child must be examined several times, and then asked if he or she would be willing to come to Fathom Sound. Only then are they permitted to come here. You were taken from your bed several times before now. While you seemed to be asleep, you would get up and sleep walk to a door or window. Then you probably began to awaken. So immediately, you were placed into a semiconscious state and then examined. At that point, you would have been very aware of your surroundings. You could communicate and function normally, except the next day you couldn't remember anything that happened the previous night.

"It was during one of these nights that you were asked

if you would be interested in spending a week learning the ways of the universe for your own benefit, and of course for the benefit of your society, and that of your planet. Some children are extremely frightened by the aliens and in those cases, no further examinations are done, and of course they are not asked to participate on Fathom Sound.

"You may ask yourself, 'How does square clouds benefit society?' They don't. The square clouds are just a side effect of a very strong presence of Devoutism on any planet. It is so strong that the very nature of things tend to occur either symmetrically, or very ordered. This orderness in nature has tremendous benefits for the planet. There are many examples of this, even on this island. One day we will take a walk, and I will point many things out to you, and explain how that process occurs.

"Most importantly, Devout Reality shows itself in society in seemingly magical ways. After you learn about Devout Reality, you will be able to recognize it in nature on Earth. Which is the reason you're here. I want you to see this, and I want you to bring this back home, Franky. I want Earth to continue its trend toward peace and harmony at an even greater rate. So much tragedy still exists there, but soon with your help, and others like you, one day Devoutism will awaken on Earth. Then, we will meet again," she said now smiling.

"Recognition is the first step. You have, many times in the past, experienced some facet of Devout Reality's effect on nature. By the way, when Devout Reality affects nature, it's called the Natural Order. Sometimes events occur with strange timing. This is called coincidence, although especially here on this planet, it is the Natural Order at work. When Moses demanded that his people go free, and they were not, it rained blood. Or did it? A very rare unstable atmospheric condition combined with an westward volcanic eruption can cause rain to be contaminated with the red ash, producing thick and very red rain drops. This can contaminate lakes and drinking holes, just as did Moses' blood rain did to those who did not free his people."

"Wait!" Franky said suddenly. "Are you saying there is no God? I mean aliens that live forever, Moses' miracle just good forecasting, miracles being coincidences . . .".

Emily smiled again. She was impressed how quickly Franky's young mind had grasped these concepts. "On the contrary. Devout Reality is the combination of religion and science. Franky, think of Devout Reality as the hand of God. Through it, all of the past, present, and future of the universe is guided. Once you understand Devout Reality, you'll realize how God interacts with you and the world around you daily. It is this goal that I have for you these next five days. It is my hope that everyone on Earth will one day not only understand Devout Reality, but practice it. And on that day, something wonderful will happen. And I'm not just talking square clouds!"

They both paused. Emily's humor seemed to keep Franky calm, even under these circumstances. A ten year old boy, on a planet light years from home would be expected to panic. But there was definitely something else at work on this island. Something made Franky feel comfortable, confident and calm. He also recognized that some other things were different. Like how he could understand concepts that would be inconceivable at home. Just like Emily said, he was smarter.

Emily stood and walked to the door, "I will be back at the crack of dawn. If you get thirsty, right outside is a stream from which you can drink. Have a good night sleep," she said as she stepped outside and closed the door.

Still sitting in this shelter of a shack, he stood up to peak out the window. Darkness had engulfed the shack village as the last remains of amber light receded toward the setting sun. Franky could see stars poking their way through the gently swaying tree tops. Further out and down the sloping landscape and through the trees, he could see what looked like a beach. Looking more carefully, he could see a definite figure standing on the beach overlooking the water. Staring off at the figure, Franky began to rethink all that Emily told him. One by one, questions appeared, some cynical, producing some doubt about what was actually happening to him. Franky decided that he would ask these questions tomorrow. In the meantime, he felt brave enough to venture out to get a closer look at the figure on the beach.

Franky slowly opened the creaking, wooden door. Peering outside, he determined that he could approach the beach with little chance of being spotted. He had some reservations about Emily's promises, and her validity. He simply needed to develop some assurances that this was neither Earth nor some purely Earthling deception. He also worried that Emily could be telling the truth, and maybe he was on some other planet. If so, would he be visited by aliens while he slept? If that were the case, was he in any danger? Despite his gut feelings, Franky was just not ready to completely give into this whole alien idea. After all, a few square clouds is hardly physical proof that he was on another planet. More than anything else, Franky wondered how much he could trust Emily, a women he just met only hours ago. In any case, he needed some outside information from a source other than Emily, regardless if it supported her claims.

Franky also had significant emotional feelings affecting his thoughts. He felt, in someway, he was familiar with this awakening routine. The dreams of the skeleton-like man that he had recently, did strike him as possibly being alien visitations, just as Emily said. So he was somewhat torn. His emotions suggested Emily was being completely honest, while his newly improved logical mind was telling him more investigation and evidence was needed.

Franky quietly stepped out of his shack and wandered down the sloping village toward the beach. Looking all around, he saw no one else. As he closed the distance, the figure gazing out at the open ocean appeared to be a human boy around his same age. The fact that the boy was a peer, made Franky feel more at ease as he approached the edge of the tree line that led directly onto the beach.

What a magnificent sight. He could say nothing, his worries eased just a little right then. It seemed they stood on the edge of the universe. Above, must have been every star in existence, he thought. The sky was so filled with stars that their combined light lit up the beach.

Franky approached the boy from behind. As he did, he discovered the reason the boy was locked into a trance. The ocean, like a rippled mirror, cast a glimmering reflection of the star filled sky above. The shine and constant sway of stars on the water surface was divided sharply by the horizon. The combination of that, with the cool soft beach sand between his toes, and the sound of the waves caressing the beach, had an immediate and strong calming effect on Franky.

Franky decided to stop about ten feet away and call to the boy. Before he could say a word, the boy spoke.

"I've never seen anything like this before. I mean, I live in California, and I have never seen a sky like this before," the boy said without turning to face Franky.

The statement caught Franky off guard as it was just

another example of someone catching his thoughts before he could put them into words. Like back on the mainland, just before boarding the helicopters Franky wondered where he was, and then got a verbal answer from another boy sitting next to him, 'We're off the coast of Fathom Sound . . .' Franky detected a strange coordination of timing affecting almost everything he thought or did. And so he stood there, speechless.

The boy finally turned to face Franky. "Where are you from?"

"Um, my name is Franky Carter. I'm from Earth, I mean New Jersey."

"My name is Troy Bolger. They tell me I'll be here for a week. You too?"

"Yeah, uh, is this your first night, Troy?"

"Yelp." Troy turned back around to the ocean and sat on the beach. He continued, "This is all pretty cool, isn't it? We're like astronauts. Look out Neil Armstrong!"

Franky walked to Troy and sat beside him. "I guess it is. I mean, if you can get over the alien part," he said causing the two to chuckle. "But really though, how much of this can you believe? I have yet to see an alien, or even a spaceship. Plus, have you seen the shacks we have to sleep in? And those helicopters were hardly shuttle crafts off the U.S.S. Enterprise! I mean, where's Spock?"

"I believe it 100%!" Troy said defiantly. "Besides, I've seen aliens, and I've seen a spaceship. Once in a while, they visit me at home when I'm asleep, and bring me to their spaceship."

Franky, wide eyed, couldn't believe his ears. "You've seen 'em? What did your parents say? You did tell them, didn't you?"

Troy paused, "Well, . . . I didn't really remember the

aliens and the spaceship until I got here. And the way I figure it, we won't remember any of this when we go back home, either."

"What did they look like?" Franky asked suddenly.

"What?"

"The aliens. What did they look like?"

"Well, they were really skinny, and a bright grey color, almost like a glowing white. They had huge dark eyes, and a little mouth. Oh, and it was really hard to tell them all apart from one another."

Franky was sure now that his dreams were significant. "I've been having dreams that a skeleton-like creature that matches your description, comes and gets me at night, and sort of tickles my stomach and back. Then, the next thing I know, it's the next day."

Troy turned to Franky. "I think it's safe to say that they were aliens. They did that tickling thing to me too. I think it is some sort of an exam. Like they're doctors or something."

Franky agreed, but he still held some reservations. "But how do we know this isn't some sort of brain washing camp or something? You saw the helicopters that brought us here. I've seen them on T.V. This whole place looks like Earth, doesn't it? Well, except the sky, and the clouds, but I mean if we were brought over in a UFO, or something, more, um, or even at least if there was an alien piloting the helicopters. You know? Something physical. Then it would be easier to believe."

Troy laid back on the beach and gazed up into the heavens. "They're UH-1's."

"What?" Franky said confused.

"UH-1's. The helicopters. They're American military choppers. My dad's in the military, and he has to fly in planes all the time. He let's me go up sometimes."

"See! Maybe that's why we haven't seen any aliens. I'll bet this is some kind of experiment by the army."

Troy shook his head. "No. I was told that alien presence here would have a bad effect on us. That we would have nightmares when we go back to Earth. And to be honest with you, I agree, they *ARE* kinda scary. How are we supposed to learn when we're afraid of the dark?"

Then all at once, all the hairs on Franky's neck stood up. He felt a wave of shock. He sensed someone behind him. Just then, an older voice froze both of the them. "Troy is right, Franky. This is all very real."

They turned to see an older human, possibly in his sixties, standing behind them. He stood there in his bare feet, wearing a black pair of shorts and a grey shirt with that same symbol that all the instructors seem to adorn. He was a black man, with grey hair cresting a severely balding head. Short grey hair ran down the sides of his face and merged at his upper lip.

"My name is Nathan, and I am a resident instructor here on Fathom Sound. You boys ought to be getting some sleep, but, considering the beauty of this beach, I can understand why you two have gone against our wishes." Nathan sat besides them then continued, "You know, Franky, there is no reason why you shouldn't doubt what Emily has told you, in fact, most people do doubt reality on their first day here on the island. It's expected. But let me assure you, you will see everyone of your doubts erased by the time you go home. I am not going to wash away your doubts here though, that will be Emily's job."

Not sure how to respond, Franky decided that it couldn't hurt to ask Nathan one question that was on his mind. "If this is all true, then why is it such a secret that this place exist? I mean, you guys go to such lengths to erase our memory of your existence, all to teach us something we will never remember. Why not have the aliens just fly down in the middle of the World Series or something and say, 'Here we are! Listen to what we have to say!'?"

Nathan looked at Franky with a smirk. "Franky's got a valid point, Troy. What do you think?"

"Oh no, I told Franky that he's wrong! I know we're on another planet!" Troy insisted despite Franky's dirty look.

"Well," Nathan started as he leaned back on the cool sand, "that is what you're gonna learn this week, young man. You see, you just can't step into a culture, a complicated society like the one that's on Earth, and say, 'Hey, this is the way it is, so live like us.'. It just doesn't work like that. A culture must develop somewhat on its own, and if it can't, it's not really mature enough to live with the terms of Devout Reality. A society must evolve to a point where it can, on its own, completely put aside pride, greed, and vengeance for the sole benefit of its citizens. We can't simply jump into everyone's television screen and announce God's arrival, let alone our version of God. No, Franky, a society, a civilization must on its own discover the virtues of Devout Reality. Fathom Sound merely represents a facilitator to that process. Then, when Earth's combined societies unite, and make strides toward Devoutism, then our society will be united with yours. Together then we will open up other civilizations on other worlds throughout the vast universe to Devout Reality."

As much as Franky held true to his doubts, he had to admit that all of this was beginning to make sense to him, and he was becoming a believer. "Nathan, I'm sorry if I question what's happening here. It's just so much, you know? I guess it will all make better sense after day five, huh?"

Troy jumped in, "Don't worry Nathan, I'll make him into a believer!"

"Will you now?" Nathan said with a laugh. "Not tonight you won't. Let's all get some sleep, come on . . .". Nathan stood and motioned the boys back to the village. They followed. As Franky entered his shack, he could feel a wave of exhaustion gripping him, and it seemed that before he hit the bed, he was fast asleep.

Franky dreamed while sleeping. He dreamed he stood in a desert. The desert floor swirled around him. The sound of thunder ripped through the air. Then from the direction of sound, rose a steady stream of smoke. His body flew up suddenly, his field of vision rising above the surface with instant acceleration, until he could see the source of the noise and smoke. It was a herd of cattle, or something that looked like cattle with longer necks. They stormed across the desert floor in perfectly formed columns, hundreds of perfectly straight rows across. They raced across the desert in perfect symmetric order. "Memphis!" he heard in his head. "Memphis!" again he barely heard. "Memphis? What's that mean?" he wondered. Even the sight of cattle marching made no sense at first, until Franky connected the square clouds to the perfect order of the herds. "This must have to do with Devout Reality," he thought.

Suddenly, he awoke. It was still dark. Franky stood up out of bed, something called to him in his head. He stepped to the door, reached out to the handle and opened the door. He was greeted by a blinding white light that completely engulfed him. As his eyes tried to adjust, he could see in the center of the light, the outline of what could possibly be an alien approaching him with it's long thin arms extended above its head. He heard a voice as it approached, calling to him, "Franky, Franky . . .".

A sudden pounding on the door woke him once again. It was a dream. Daylight invaded the cracks of the door, and he heard Emily calling on the other side, "Franky, are you going to wake up?" Finally, she pushed open the door. "Hey, sleepyhead, I see you made to day two."

Chapter Two

Defining Virtue

"No metal can, No not the hangman's ax, bear half the keenness of thy sharp envy."

> *-William Shakespeare*
> *"The Merchant of Venice"*
> *IV,i,123.*

October 16, 1976.
7:00 a.m.

Emily looked at Franky's tired face. "Come on, let's get something to eat," she said tugging at his shirt sleeve.

Franky rubbed his eyes, looked down and noticed that he was still in the same clothes as the previous night - grey sweat pants and shirt.

Emily seemed to know what Franky was thinking. "Don't worry about getting your clothes dirty, you'll have some clean clothes sitting on your bed by the time we get back from breakfast."

"Oh, how's that?" he asked.

"Some of the instructors have already eaten, so while you and the other students eat, they'll go around and place clean clothing in each room," she said while gesturing for Franky to stand.

Emily and Franky stepped out of the shack. Franky squinted to the early morning, warm, orange beam of sunlight. Looking around at each shack scattered across the hillside, he could see that many of the other instructors and students had already begun to walk down toward the beach.

They began to walk down the sloping hillside. Suddenly, the strangeness of the island's vegetation caught his attention. Some plants, like large green helium balloons, floated gently with the morning breeze. They were rooted to a dark green vine. Occasionally, the island breezes pushed the balloon plants casually into one another, causing them to make a soft humming sound.

"Wow!" Franky yelled pointing toward a few. "What do you call those?"

"Well, on this island, we all call them balloon plants."

Franky walked up to one, "Can I touch it?"

"Just be gentle," Emily said as she walked up along side of him. "They are very shy."

Franky had nearly touched one when he yanked his hand back. "Shy? They are plants. Aren't they?"

Emily raised her eyebrows and put her hands on her hips. "Franky, you need to open your mind to everything you experience here."

Franky looked back confused.

Emily then pulled Franky back away from one of the plants and then clapped her hands suddenly together. Instantly all of the surrounding balloon plants roared as they quickly deflated and fell to the ground.

"You see, Franky. These plants are shy. When the sun comes up in the morning, chemical reactions occur within the plants root system, which creates a gas that is lighter than air. This gas rises up the hollow vine and into the plant's large membrane, the balloon part. This way, as the membrane enlarges, it can soak up more sunlight, which allows the plant to store more energy from the sun. They deflate when they sense possible danger, like wild animals or stormy weather."

Emily tugged on Franky's shirt sleeve. "Come on, we're gonna be late for breakfast."

They again began to walk down the sloping hillside trail that lead to the beach. "So, Nathan tells me you went for a walk last night," she said with a smirk.

"Well, I wouldn't call it a walk. I just wanted to see the beach," he said defensively.

"Okay, look, I don't mind you going for walks, or going to the beach, but, you really ought to tell me first. Deal?"

Franky nodded, "Deal."

Just then, they stepped out of the trees and onto the beach. Down closer to the water, were several rows of wooden picnic tables adorn with mounds of food. Most of the students had already started eating. "What's for breakfast, anyhow?" he asked.

"I sure hope you're hungry, cause we believe in a big breakfast."

"Hungry? I'm so hungry I could eat a horse," Franky said as he picked up his pace toward the tables.

"You won't find horse on the menu here. In fact, you won't find any kind of meat on the menu. We are all vegetarians. I know you aren't, but for the next five days I just want you to see what it's like, okay?"

"How about eggs?" he asked.

"No, usually for breakfast we eat fruit and something like oatmeal," she said.

"What kind of fruit?"

"Some are kinds you would recognize. Like bananas, or plums. But for the most part, you've never seen anything like it before."

Many students were already eating as they arrived to the tables. After greeting some of the students and instructors, Franky and Emily sat next to each other. Sitting directly across the table was Troy and Nathan.

The table was loaded with wooden bowls filled with odd looking foods. Each place setting consisted of a wooden plate, and cup. Utensils were made of an extraordinarily light metallic material that was also incredibly shiny.

Franky recognized that the group he was seated with was the same that was in the helicopter. Each student appeared to be seated next to their instructor. When Franky took note of what others around him were eating, he found that the students were eating only recognizable fruits from Earth, while the instructors ate a variety.

Franky reached for a fruit he'd never seen before. This immediately drew some stares from students around the table. He bravely plopped the giant tomato looking thing on his plate. Aware of his attentive audience, he lifted his glittering, weightless knife, and whispered to Emily, "Em, what is this thing?"

"It's a Saladgate Air Fruit," she whispered back.

"Yummm," he said sarcastically as he poked his knife into the giant red produce. Franky immediately noticed that the skin was tougher than he expected. He pressed harder. As the blade finally pierced it's skin, a sudden rush of air poured out of the fruit, deflating it to a dried up looking flat tomato on his plate. At once, the entire group of students roared into laughter.

Franky looked up at Emily with his mouth open. "Uh, what do I do with it now?"

"Use it as a frisbee!" a boy yelled out causing another roar of laughter.

"Just wait," Emily said now smiling.

With that, the fruit suddenly began to inflate inself, silencing the group. Some of the nearby students even gasped in horror and leaned away. Franky quickly raised up his knife as an expression of shock and fear gripped his face. Ready to do battle with the fruit, Emily quickly grabbed the knife out of his hand, and said, "Just watch."

The fruit inflated to its original size, stopped, quivered, and then stopped again. Suddenly, it split open into four equal parts, and as the skin fell back to the plate, the bright pink interior became exposed. In what was once the center of the fruit, was what Franky could only describe as a bird bath shaped structure filled with a brown liquid. At the base of this structure was what looked like tiny orange grapes.

"Dip the grapes into the juice and taste it," said Emily.

The entire group watched in amazement as Franky did just that. And as his eyes lit up, his hand quickly reached for another indicating his immense approval. At once, every student jumped up and grabbed their own Saladgate Air Fruit.

After breakfast, Franky begged Emily that he be permitted to bring home some seeds of his new found fruit. Of course, Emily immediately refused the request.

"You know you can never bring anything from here home with you," she remarked. "Besides, you'd wake up the next morning with these seeds in your hand, or in your pocket, and say, 'Gee, what are these things doing in my pocket?', and you'd throw them away. Remember, you're not going to consciously remember any of this."

"Sorry, I was just asking," he said as he hung his head down. "Em, I don't want to forget!"

"I know. Nobody ever wants to forget. But it's vital to this program. If you go back home and remember this, everybody will think that you're crazy. But let's just assume you convince everyone that this all really happened. Then what? Is everyone going to say, 'Hey, lets all practice Devout Reality!' I don't think so. This program is geared to alter the way human emotions affect their actions in subconscious ways. I'm talking about emotions like pride, greed and vengeance. This is the kind of stuff we're going to learn today. So lets get going."

They stood up and walked back toward Franky's shack. Upon entering, Franky noticed the clothing sitting on his bed, just as Emily said it would be. "Don't put those on yet. In a little while you'll have time to do that."

Emily walked over to the blackboard, picked up a piece of chalk and drew a circle. Next to the circle she drew four straight lines intersecting one another at the same point, which was the midpoint of each line.

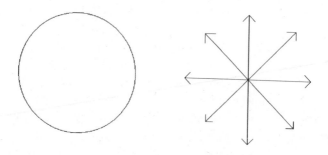

"Do you know what these figures represent?" Emily asked.

"Well," Franky said slowly. "One is a circle and the other is a star."

"From now on, think of the circle as nature around people, and think of the star as nature around animals and plants," Emily said.

Franky looked puzzled. "Nature?"

"Yes. The thing I want you to understand is that nature reacts and interacts with people, animals, trees, plants, the weather, and everything else on the planet."

"I thought nature was all those things," Franky said confused.

"You're right," Emily said smiling. "You and me, and the trees outside, and even this shack are part of nature.

And so, we all affect, and interact with one another. That's called the Natural Order. We all work, play and live within it."

"Okay, I understand that part. But what do stars and circles have to do with nature?" Franky asked.

"Well, let me finish. You see, Franky. This whole week is going to be devoted to teaching you about the complexities of that interaction process. When a tree falls in the woods, hundreds of miles away, as insignificant as that may seem, it affects you in some way. Before you go home, Franky, you will know exactly how."

Franky looked back to the chalkboard, still confused about how the shapes had anything to do with the Natural Order. Emily seemed to know what he was thinking.

"The circle," Emily said suddenly. "It represents people. While the star represents animals and plants. People, because they are sentient, that is to say, conscious and self aware, interact with the Natural Order differently than animals and plants.

"Similarly, the decisions conscious beings make on a day to day basis have less to do with natural instinct than they do with society. For example, if back home, you want to have money, you know that you have to perform a task."

"Like a job?" Franky asked.

"Yes, like a job. There is a give and take system in place. That's called the Social Order. Meanwhile, animals and plants, simply react exclusively on instincts. When the lion roars, animals in her way don't stop and think, they run!"

Emily pointed to the center of the star. "This is the animal or plant, and the arrows represent all the things that happen to that animal or plant. Whether it be a good meal or a bad injury, things happen. And what I am suggesting to you is that in the animal world all things happen at random. The lion may be lucky one day, and the next, be someone else's meal. There is no guiding natural intervention in the animal and plant world order."

"So, are you saying that something is guiding our lives?" Franky asked.

Emily was happy to see Franky understand these concepts so quickly. "Yes, exactly!" she said excitedly. "The more a Social Order acts outside of basic natural instincts, the less things occur at random, and the more Devout Reality affects nature. It's a never ending cycle. That's what the circle represents. The flowing cycle of the give and take process."

"Devout Reality affects nature? You mean, like square clouds?" Franky asked.

"Yes! Except, a Social Order must be very, very well ordered before Devout Reality will affect nature to the degree where clouds become symmetrical," Emily responded.

"So, to be very ordered, people can't use their instincts?" Franky asked.

Emily chuckled, "Well, sort of, yes. Many human instincts are great for survival on the open plain when the only thing protecting him or her is a spear. These are instincts that cause a deepening of emotions like pride, greed, and vengeance. Pride tends to make people selfish. It's a 'Look what I have,' or 'Look what I've accomplished,' mentality. This mentality tends to keep people and societies from truly coming together, and it hinders the give and take process. Greed follows a similar path. This mentality says, 'Get as much as you can, and then keep it.' And finally, there is vengeance, which is to say, 'Get back at who or whatever took from you.' And unfortunately, these emotions run through all of us. They are woven into our very spirit. And while some people have more or less of one or another, none of us, no matter how hard we try, will ever completely break free from these negative emotions that makes us all human beings."

"So what's the point?" Franky asked.

"You mean of this class? And of this week?"

"Yeah. Then why are we here? What good is it going to do?"

"Because these classes are making a difference back on Earth. People are changing. Millions of years ago, the aliens that brought you here had similar emotions within their species. Their society, and very species eventually rose above that. Now, they live in harmony with nature."

"I still don't understand. How does living in harmony with nature help anyone? I mean, who needs square clouds?" Franky asked.

Emily looked back at the blackboard. "That's where these shapes come into play." She then picked up an eraser and wiped out the left and right sides of the circle. She then drew a dot on each side, then an arrow symbol above the left dot, and below the right dot.

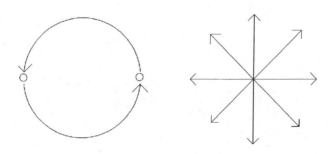

Emily then pointed to the star. "This is how nature is under normal circumstances. You never know what's going to come or go. Things happen at anytime, and completely at random." She then pointed back to the circle, "This is how random nature is around self aware species with a maximum ordered Social Order that is large in population. Nature follows a specific pattern. It basically compliments the give and take process."

"Well, how close is Earth. I mean, how ordered is our society?" Franky asked.

Emily took the eraser and quickly erased the star. She then drew two more circles on either side of the original circle.

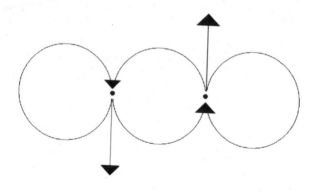

"This is generally how most societies on Earth look today. But as time goes on, the Earth's Social Orders have slowly become closer and closer to the very well ordered model. I think that soon Earth will reach that point."

"But how does nature change?" he asked.

Emily pointed to the drawing, "This model represents

something called a polis. One dot represents a citizen, while the other represents his or her society. A very well ordered society will always have the citizen giving to his or her society, while the society is giving back to the citizen."

"The give and take process," Franky blurted out.

"Exactly," Emily said. "Today, on Earth, much of the citizens only give to the society through taxes or jobs to earn money. When people can, they give to themselves. That's why there are two extra circles to the Earth polis, people are giving to themselves. And the reason people give to themselves is because of the three emotions, pride, greed and vengeance."

"Hold up! Let me see if I got this right. You're saying that the square clouds are caused by nature. And that nature forced the clouds to become ordered because the people around here, on this planet, are very well ordered?" Franky asked.

"Yes. Basically, anytime you have a city with lots of people who together give to each other without thought to themselves, and they do this for a significant period of time, nature around that polis changes.

"How can that be? How does nature know that people are giving to one another?"

"Well, there is an entire science behind it. We will go into detail about that before the end of the week, but basically, it has everything to do with the fact that people are self aware beings. They have a conscious intelligence. You see, Franky, consciousness affects reality. On a tiny scale at first. You know what an atom is?"

"Yeah. It's what we're all made of," Franky said smiling.

"That's right," Emily said. "But did you know that there are tiny particles that make up atoms?"

"I think so. I seem to know that, somehow. But I'm not sure where I learned it."

"And there are still smaller particles that make up those particles. These are protons, electrons, neutrons, quarks, and so on. There are more types of small particles then there are people on this island. But, my point is that on the smallest scale, these subatomic particles react to conscious intelligence. Normally, these subatomic particles act at random, changing their spin, rotation, direction, and so on. However, when a conscious intelligence, surrounding these particles, is very well ordered, then they too become ordered. That's when they loose their randomness. Once that happens over a vast area, the combined effect of ordered subatomic particles on atoms and molecules, and thus plants, and animals, is order, symmetry, and predictability within nature."

"So, when nature becomes ordered, it forces non-self aware animals, plants and sometimes the weather to become ordered. But how does that help people?" Franky asked again.

Emily was amazed and over joyed at how quickly Franky picked up the lesson. "Wow! That is the whole point of today's lesson. When those things become ordered, events happening to people occur in an ordered fashion also. So, if I was a person always giving something to another, I shall receive something back in the same value. This is not a new idea, not even on Earth. There are many words for this, Karma is one. Piety is another. If you didn't understand a thing about the lesson I just taught you, understand that there is a science to Karma. That science is called Devout Reality."

Emily stood up. "Lets go for a walk. You change into some clean clothes, and I'll wait outside. I want to show you what I mean."

Franky quickly changed into the all grey sweat suit and exited his shack. Emily gestured him to follow as she began to walk across the village in a direction away from the beach. As they walked, Franky noticed that all the students he saw wore the same color sweat suit as he - grey.

"Why are all the clothes grey?" he asked.

"Not all the clothes are grey, Franky. Just the ones you've seen so far," she replied.

It seemed a little odd to him, but on the other hand, so did being on another planet. Franky decided not to pursue a more specific answer, even if it was strange.

"Where are we going?" he asked as they started to climb an inclined trail.

"You'll see," she said picking up the pace.

The path grew steep, and it became obvious that they were hiking the lower base of one of the mountains. The trees were very unusual to Franky. There were no branches, except for at the very top where all the branches stuck out like spokes on a bicycle tire. In between each spoke was what looked like a yellowish leafy material. The leafy material covered the entire circular top of the tree so that it looked like a twenty foot tall yellow umbrella.

"These trees, they look like . . ." Franky said as he paused to glance up at one again.

Emily finished his sentence, "I know, I know. Like giant umbrellas, right?"

"Yeah, like umbrellas. What is it with this place? Balloons, umbrellas, what's next, parachutes?"

Emily giggled. "No, but these are really neat trees. Take a look at the trunk," she said as they stepped over to one of the tree trucks. Emily pointed to what looked like several sets of thick vines that extended up to the canopy above. "These vines are like our muscles. At night, they will contract and pull this tree's canopy down. And tomorrow morning, a chemical reaction within the tree will cause water to fill up sacks that are near the top of the tree. When the sacks fill up, they will sink part way down the tree, causing the canopy to open - much like an umbrella does."

Franky noticed that the umbrella trees grew close together, and because of their canopies partially overlapping, very little sunlight got through to the forest floor.

"Are they all yellow?" he asked.

"No. Come with me and you'll see them from above," she said as they starting again up the trail.

In a short while, they broke out of the trees and onto a soft green plateau. Tall lush grass swayed to the soft winds. Emily lead Franky across the plateau until they stood near the edge of a cliff that overlooked the village, forest, and beach.

Like an impressionist painting of a multicolored flower bed, the umbrella trees stretched out for miles below them. Their colors varied from yellow to green, purple, red, and orange. The sky above seemed to be bluer than Earth's. Franky looked out over the ocean. He could barely make out the mainland across the water. Evenly spaced, perfectly shaped clouds marched smoothly across the sky.

"There must be a lot of people on this planet," Franky said softly.

"Billions," she replied.

"Are they aliens?"

"Nah. They're just people," Emily said with a grin.

"Humans?"

"Not really. Is it important that you know?"

"No. I was just curious. Just tell me, do they look like humans?"

"Yes, but they're not exactly human."

"So they are aliens," Franky said as he turned toward her.

"No. They're related to humans. They're sort of like part human. Look, unless this is important, I'd rather not go into this," she said.

"Ok," Franky said sure that he wouldn't bring it up again. But then in the distance he could see a glimmer of sun on the mainland. It looked like it could be a reflection off a structure. "What's that?" he said pointing to the glare.

"That's a city," Emily said after squinting her eyes.

"Oh. What's it called?"

"Memphis," she replied.

Franky paused. 'Memphis?' he thought. That was the word he heard in his dreams last night. He wondered what the significance of that could be.

"I'll bet it's beautiful," he said.

"That's what I hear."

"You've never been there?" he said hardly believing his ears.

"No. But it's very old. Hundreds of thousands of years old. Keep in mind Franky, that modern man on Earth has only been around for a little over 30,000 years. Memphis is many times that age."

Franky thought about it for a little while before something very odd hit him. He wondered how the race of people living there could be hundreds of the thousands of years old while modern man on Earth was only 30,000 years old. "Em, how could. . . " he started before being interrupted.

"I know what you're going to ask. That's why I didn't

want to talk about it. Franky, humans are a result of aliens tinkering with the genetic make-up of pre-modern man beings. About 90,000 years ago, aliens decided to tone down the instinctual emotions of neanderthals. This is what lead to the creation of people as you know them. Their genetic make-up had to be altered to remove those negative emotions we talked about. This tinkering of genetics takes hundreds, even thousands of years."

"So, aliens wanted to create humans so that Devout Reality could be born on Earth?" he asked.

"Well, not exactly. Alien tinkering with human genetics continues today," she said softly.

"So, what does that mean? Are people in Memphis, like half human, half neanderthal?" he asked confused.

"Uh, no. This is the hard part. They're the next generation of humans. In effect, the next evolutionary step of human beings."

"What? Why are they here then? Why aren't they on Earth?" he asked confused.

"Some are!" she answered quickly. "Over the last forty years, aliens have been introducing the first step of their genetic code into many human's DNA."

"Are they smarter, or something?" he asked.

"No. Humans don't need to be any smarter then they are already. The new generation of humans will have different mental discipline. Basically, their emotions will be less dramatic."

"Like pride, greed, and vengeance?" Franky asked.

"Yes. Those emotions are subdued. So, as you can see, Fathom Sound's program to initiate Devout Reality on Earth is only one part of a large and complex operation."

Emily then pulled out of a small bag that was tied around her waist, a rolled up piece of paper. "Here, I want you to put this on your sweat shirt," she said while unrolling it. She then handed it to Franky.

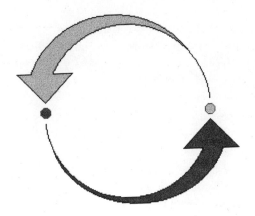

"The red colored arrow goes on top, while the blue on the bottom. This is the polis symbol, and when you wear it on the upper left handed side of your shirt, it means you understand Devout Reality, and will practice it."

"But I'm not sure I know how I can practice it," Franky said as Emily placed the symbol on the front of his shirt. As she did, it somehow quickly absorbed into the fabric.

"Well, you know the basics already, and we're only into day two of your lessons. That's quite an accomplishment, I'd say. Tomorrow, I will start to go over how nature is altered by a very well ordered Social Order. The following day, we will do whatever you want - go hiking, smimming, or whatever," she said as she stepped back to look at Franky wearing his new emblem.

"Can we go to Memphis?" he interrupted.

Emily paused and thought a moment, "Uh, I'm not sure.

Maybe. I'll let you know tomorrow, okay?"

"That would be great if we could," he said excitedly.

"And on day five, we'll review, then after dinner you will go back home."

The rest of the afternoon, they sat on the edge of the cliff, admiring the island's beauty. Franky reflected on the events of the last two days. But mostly, he couldn't help feeling frustrated about the prospect of losing his memory of these five days on Fathom Sound.

Emily pulled from the ground some plants that looked like radishes. She showed Franky how to peel the skin off the vegetable and eat it. Together, they made a lunch of the surrounding plants. Emily pulled up a water filled sack from a small young umbrella tree, and shared the liquid with Franky. Franky was amazed how it tasted like lemonade.

"I have to confess, Franky, the umbrella trees are really called, pal pa trees. And the balloon plants are called, sol pa plants. But, for so many years, children like yourself called them what they look like to you, and the new names stuck," Emily said as she took another swig of the juice in the sack.

"Em, if Devout Reality favors Social Orders that avoid those negative emotions, why do so many bad people succeed?" Franky asked wiping his face with his sleeve.

"That's a good question. That's something we're going to talk about tomorrow. But, I will say this now, throughout Earth's history, there have been thousands of Social Orders. Monarchies, and Dictatorships that oppressed the citizenry. And one by one, each eventually collapsed. Now, the world is full of free nations that are thriving in world peace. Earth is changing for the better."

Franky gathered his thoughts of the day's lesson as he

and Emily began their hike back to the village. Even Franky was amazed that his comprehension was occurring so easily. Maybe it was the island. Emily did say that his mind was somehow altered.

While making their way down the mountain, Emily told Franky that dinner was going to be held on a boat. She said that most of the other students would also be there. Franky imagined that the boat would have to be huge to hold so many people.

They arrived back to the village. Franky immediately noticed that very few of the students had the logo that he wore on his shirt. The fact that Franky had the logo on his shirt, drew stares. This made Franky feel proud, but uncomfortable. They walked past about a dozen or so shacks until they found a path that led through the trees. The sun was on its way down, so the forest began to take on a darker look. After a short walk, a clearing began to materialize before them.

They stepped out of the forest and onto the beach. Emily stopped. "There's the ship," she said pointing toward a massive ship docked to a pier. Both the pier and ship were made of wood. Its two huge sails flapped faintly in the distance.

They again started walking toward the ship. When they made it to the pier, Franky could see that most of the students were already on board. Emily and Franky stepped onto the deck of the great ship, and he immediately spotted Troy talking to another boy. Emily told him that he was welcome to explore the ship, or gather with the other students. Franky took that as a cue, and walked over to Troy.

"Oh, hi Franky," Troy said as he saw him weaving through the crowd of grey sweat suit wearing students gathered on the main deck.

"Franky, this is Emmanuel. He's from Canada," Troy said now staring at the logo on Franky's shirt. "Hey, what's that?" he asked.

"Just a logo, that's all. It just means that I understood today's lesson," Franky explained.

"I wonder why we didn't get one," Emmanuel mused.

Emmanuel was like every other student in that he was under the age of fourteen.

"Who is your instructor?" Franky asked Emmanuel.

"Her name is Mary. She's the one with a brown robe at the front. See her?" he asked while pointing in a crowd of instructors. "The one with the brown hair. . .in a pony tail."

Franky nodded after spotting her. He noticed that Emmanuel had a slight accent, and he began to wonder about the different languages on Earth. He then turned to both Troy and Emmanuel and asked, "Do any of you guys know if there are any students who don't speak English?"

Troy immediately said that there were none. "Nathan told me that each five day camp is grouped according to language, and by instructors who speak the language of that particular group.

Suddenly, the ship moved. Ropes holding the giant ship had been removed, and the sails filled with the sunsetting winds. With the movement, all of the students quickly took positions along the sides so that they could gain a better view. On the horizon, the red sun slowly began to dip into the ocean. The wonderful smell of the ocean surrounding Franky, forced him to take a deep breath. Gently cutting through the calm waters, the ship set off toward open sea. The sky above turned darker, exposing that amazing nighttime sight of uncountable stars once again. Only this time, Troy and Franky found themselves completely surrounded by water. The twinkling stars above reflected on the water all around for as far as either of them could see. The tiny lights on the rippled surface cast a silence on all the students. Quiet beauty held everyone spellbound.

It was during the trance-like moment that Franky experienced a vision. A flash of a faded memory spread across his eyes as he gazed of into the ocean. The reflecting star filled sky reminded him of a mirror. It must have been that reflection that the faded memory came back to him.

The room was oval, and entirely sterile white. The walls rose thirty or forty feet up, until they angled inward at 45 degrees, then suddenly leveled off to form a ceiling. The angled part of the walls that connected to the ceiling was made of tinted windows. Franky laid on a table, face up. Most of his body was covered with a thin, white sheet. He could feel a slight numbing pain in the back of his head. He reached back there and to his shock, found a wire! Turning his head to the side, he followed the wire with his eyes. The wire ran from the back of his head and into the white wall. Then immediately next to the wire, another wire came out of the wall and ran into another person's head, who was laying directly next to him. Franky then looked into the face of the person next to him as he looked with open eyes back at Franky. It was himself! Or, he quickly thought, maybe a twin. Whatever the case, he was very frightened by the situation, so he immediately turned his head back forward, and looked back up at the ceiling.

Through the tinted windows, Franky could begin to see figures standing all around the room above. They appeared to be staring down on the two boys. Slight movement from a few of the figures drew his attention on them. Fear suddenly gripped him as he focused. They were not human. He could make out a very large head, with large dark eyes.

The creatures were skinny with light colored bodies. He naturally began to tremble, and was near shock when this memory faded once again.

"Franky!" called a voice.

Franky shook off the gaze. He thought, maybe he was seeing himself. Maybe there was a mirror dividing the room in half. He assumed that the person next to him was just a reflection.

"Yo, Franky. Over here!" Troy yelled from behind.

Franky turned around and noticed that all of the students were now sitting at tables set up on the main deck. Troy and Emmanuel left him a place to sit at their table.

A very thick lettuce like salad, presented in a clear bowl was everyone's dinner. As expected, the young students moaned at the thought of a completely green dinner, however, everyone seemed to enjoy it.

"Good evening everyone," Nathan said as the group turned toward him. Standing on an elevated part of the ship, Nathan addressed the group. "My name is Nathan. I am the lead instructor here on Fathom Sound. I hope all of your lessons on Devout Reality went well. But just in case some of you are a little unclear about today's lesson, I want to answer your questions, and discuss a few things about it. You know, you heard a lot today about pride, greed and vengeance. About how these emotions can be counter productive in any attempt to harmonize a Social Order with the Natural Order. It can be confusing, why you are here, how can this all help?

"Let me put an end to your confusion. To practice Devout Reality, it is this simple. Give. Give to a stranger a courteous, 'hello.' Give to a friend all of your heart, your unquestioning trust, your time, your unwavering loyalty, and your very home. And finally, give to your enemy your love. For then, you no longer will have any enemies.

"You have all had a long day, and I know it has been hard being away from home. But I'm here to tell you that these lessons are making a difference on Earth, albeit a slow process. And yes, there is a lot of physics behind Devout Reality, some of it you will learn. But in the end, there is but one thing to do - give. Give in all of your actions, strategies, and thoughts. Be kind, and loving to all. And not just to people. To all things, living or not.

"And through those actions, your will be rewarded. And as a Social Order, that gives as a whole, Devout Reality will be forged. The forces within nature that cause change, will cease, and predictability will prevail. And when that happens, the perfect polis will be formed, and planet Earth will see the power and benefits of Devout Reality. Are there any questions?"

A young girl raised her hand, "What if giving to someone is taking from another?"

"You mean like Robin Hood?" he asked as the girl shook her head.

"Look, giving and taking should never be put in the same sentence. A perfect polis depends on every member of the Social Order, collectively working together to give. It is not going to work if only half of the population is working toward that goal. Individually, each of you must give back to the Social Order. You can not worry about who is giving what, and to whom. Go about your lives with the satisfaction that you personally give in everything you do. And I'm not just talking about money. On this planet, there is no such thing as money. When I speak of giving, I am talking about your actions. What you do for other people. Give, not because you expect something in return, but because it is the *RIGHT* thing to do!

"What Robin Hood did was wrong. He took from someone. Never take, regardless of the reason. Now if everyone in Robin Hood's Social Order was giving to each other, there would have been no reason for what he did. You see, right and wrong must be determined by the give and take system - the polis. To give is right, to take is wrong. It's that simple."

Nathan paused and looked around the ship for a moment until he spotted Franky. "Franky, come up here," he said while waving him forward.

Surprised, Franky stood up slowly, and then began to weave his way to Nathan. A soft mumble grew from the crowd of students as Franky cut through their stares. When he finally reached Nathan, Nathan turned him around so that Franky faced the students. Nathan then pointed at the polis logo on his shirt. "You all know what this is, right?"

"Yes, but how come we don't have a shirt like that?" someone yelled out.

"Are you jealous?" Nathan answered back.

There was no response. "I'll take that as a 'yes.' The moment all of you saw this logo on this student's shirt, you wanted one of your own. That's those negative emotions all of you must learn to control. Be happy that Franky has the shirt with the logo. Don't desire it, and you will succeed in this first test."

After answering a few more questions, Nathan retired the group. The great ship docked and unloaded the students. Emily escorted Franky back to his shack, and once again, Franky fell asleep unusually fast.

In his dreams, he saw a mountain, and behind it a golden colored pyramid, with a doorway that had blinding light escaping from within it. Above the doorway was engraved the polis symbol. Strangely enough, the whole complex looked familiar to him. Not like he remembered the Egyptian pyramids from books, but like he had been there before. He could not explain what many of these feelings were caused from. He wondered if he was ever there at the pyramid . . . or, was it just a dream.

Chapter Three

The Dreamland Alliance

"When spider webs unite, they can tie up a lion."

-Ethiopian Proverb

October 17, 1976.
9:00 a.m.

After breakfast, Emily and Franky went back to his shack to continue his lessons. As Emily promised, day three was geared toward the actual mechanics of Devout Reality. Today, he figured, he'd learn how Devout Reality physically alters nature around a well ordered Social Order. How clouds form perfect squares, and how exactly that would benefit people.

One thing occurred to him that he didn't want to reveal to Emily. He wished so much that he could retain his memory of this week, and his search for a way had begun. He thought, maybe if he could remember just one thing, it should be grounded in science. That way, if he did remember later, he would have at least some kind of evidence of his journey.

So when Emily drew the structure of the universe on the blackboard, he studied every curve, and every detail. He listened to Emily explain how the universe constantly expands until gravitational forces curve the expanding space-time back around onto a narrowing realm. Like a funnel, space-time then forces all of the universes planets, stars, and galaxies back into a single collapsed point, causing a rebirth of the universe. This pattern of birth, death, and rebirth of the universe is a cycle, Emily said, that has no beginning and will have no end.

Franky was determined to remember this image. Even after they returned from lunch, Franky held the memory of the universe's shape in his head, hoping he'd never forget it.

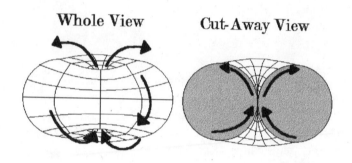

Whole View   **Cut-Away View**

In the afternoon, Emily shifted to the main topic.

"Let me first say that there are many degrees in which nature is affected around any Social Order, whether or not it is well ordered or poorly ordered," she said.

"But yesterday you said that only a well ordered Social Order affects nature," Franky said confused.

"And I stand by that. But there are two types of well ordered Social Orders, and all others fall in between," Emily said as she drew a new figure on the board. "As you can see, Social Orders can be anywhere along this line," she said pointing to the 'Degree of Order' line. "Nature is normally in a state of disorder. Which is a five. This is how nature is under most circumstances. However, as soon as you put a self aware, conscious species within any Natural Order, nature will change depending on how well

ordered the Social Order. Between a five and nine, nature
is altered to become ordered, more ordered the closer to nine
the Social Order is."

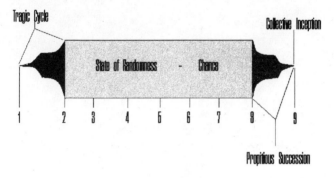

DEGREE OF ORDER LINE

"What is this planet?" he asked.

"It's a nine. Square clouds will only form with a nine or
one," she answered.

"Oh, but also with a one?" he said confused.

"Yes. On the lower side of the scale, nature becomes
more ordered as the Social Order becomes more ordered the
other way. Instead of a giving system, a take/steal system
exists, where pride, greed, and vengeance is valued. Under
a Social Order of one, there is absolutely no giving to
anything or anyone. But don't worry, societies like that
quickly dissolve, usually tragically."

"So, how does that make Social Orders of nine different
from ones if both are well ordered?" he asked.

"It's a cycle. Look at your shirt. Because nature is
reacting in an orderly fashion, it will do so according to the
Social Order around it. So, the Natural Order will respond

in a giving way around Social Orders of nine, and in a taking way around Social Orders of a one," she said pointing to a drawling of a Social Order - One.

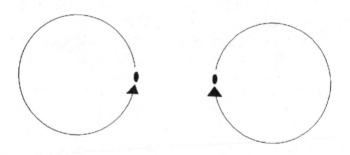

"Most Earth Social Orders are currently between a three and a six. Which means for the most part that the Natural Order is not affected by human consciousness on Earth. Nature on Earth tends towards disorder, where randomness is a factor.

"What about animals?" he asked.

"All non-conscious animals are just a part of the Natural Order itself. So, they will always be a five. Now, between four and six, nature acts mainly disordered. All events will then occur as a function of chance, this is especially the case at five. So, it is obvious then that the higher a Social Order is along the line, the more beneficial nature will act around that society. Between a one and three, Social Orders have entered a tragic cycle to which there is no escape. Once a Social Order enters this downward spiral, there will be a collapse of that society.

"Between a seven and a nine, the Social Order enters an upward spiral. This is called a 'propitious succession.' There is also no escape from this cycle. A Social Order will continue to trend to the point where the polis becomes perfectly well ordered. Keep in mind though, that it may take hundreds of years for a Social Order to get from a seven to a nine, or a three to a one. Tomorrow, you will see first hand what a Social Order of the magnitude of nine is like! When you see Memphis," she said with a smile.

"I can go!" Franky said excitedly.

Emily nodded.

"I can't wait!" he said. "You're going with me, right?"

"Of course. But you must promise to do as I say once we are there. We don't want to cause too much of a stir," she said seriously.

"Can Troy go with us?"

"Well, I'm going to have to ask his instructor, but I'm sure they would like to go as well."

"So we're going to Memphis. By the way, what is this planet called anyway?" he asked just realizing that he was never told.

"Dreamland," she replied.

"Dreamland?" he said with a funny look. "Seems like a strange name."

"The sky was growing dark once again. Emily took Franky down the same path that lead to the plateau where he first saw Memphis. They hiked up the base of the mountain until they reached the familiar plateau. By that time the sun had nearly set. Stepping toward the cliff Franky was amazed at the beauty of the sun's dark red glow. Slowly, stars popped up around the great red ball of fire as the ocean snuffed out the last light from its rays.

"Step closer to the edge," she said.

"I'm afraid of heights," he replied nervously.

"I want you to see something. Here, take my hand," she said as she held her hand out to him.

Franky slowly reached out and took her hand. He then took two cautious steps toward the edge. "What is it?" he asked looking down the cliff.

"There," she said pointing toward the water near the beach. "There it is again!" she said excitedly.

Franky looked at the ocean. Suddenly, a glowing neon green streak appeared under the water. It darted rapidly away from the direction of the setting sun and toward the beach where it seemingly vanished. Several waves of the spectacle occurred. "What are they?" he asked.

"Not they, but what is it," she responded.

"Huh?" he moaned confused.

"You mean, what is it. It's not alive. It's a side effect of the Natural Order around a magnitude nine Social Order. At this time of night, and from this height, you will see this on every beach on Dreamland."

Franky looked across to the shimmering city lights of Memphis. There was something captivating about the city. Maybe it was that voice in his dreams. He couldn't explain his fascination with Memphis, he just knew he had to go there.

The sunset was complete, revealing the most stunning view Franky had yet seen. "Wow," he said aloud while gazing at the stars and ocean.

"Yeah, wow," Emily agreed.

Then, one by one, a popping sound shot out from the forest below as each umbrella plant closed it's canopy for the night. The forest seemed to come alive with movement as the popping sound increased into a fireworks like crackling.

"Thank you, Em," he said as he turned toward her. "For everything here. You know, despite what you say, I'm going to remember you, and this island."

Emily looked down at her feet. "Everyone says that, you know."

"But I'm not everyone," he said looking back up at the stars.

Emily stared down on Franky, causing him to turn back toward her. Emily looked into his serious eyes. Squinting, as if she could read his mind. For a second, she believed him. And then she looked back out into the ocean. "I don't think so," she finally said.

"Did anyone ever get back to Earth and remember? Has it ever happened?" he asked.

"That's a tough question. Like I told you, you will remember everything subconsciously, and nothing consciously. Only over time will little things emerge."

"Yeah, but, did anyone ever remember everything right from the get go?" he asked again.

"No. Not like that. And even if they did, who'd believe them? But there are those who remember little pieces of this or that. Especially of the abduction process. Things that are frightening to people are sometimes harder to erase from their memories," she admitted.

"Does anyone on Earth know about Fathom Sound?"

Emily paused. "That's where things get kind of complicated," she said after taking a deep breath. "As you know, all former students deep inside know about Fathom Sound. Other then that, there are a few select individuals who know about the entire alien program of Devout Reality."

"There are!" Franky said realizing instantly its significance.

"Yes."

"Who? The President?" he guessed.

"No. There's a hand full of people in the world who know. It's a very long story," she said hoping in vain he would not pursue the question. But as she looked into his face, Emily quickly realized that this was a question he would not let go. "In 1947 an alien ship crashed in the desert in New Mexico. Aliens had been observing humans for thousands of years, and at that time, the aliens were particularly interested in the United States technological advancement in the field of nuclear science and the testing of atomic weapons, which were being done in New Mexico. This crash was not the way the aliens would have liked to introduce themselves to the human race, however, it was obviously not by choice. All of the alien crew died. The military quickly became involved in the ship's recovery.

"President Truman, of the United States, and a guy named Hillenkoetter, as well as several military personnel were privy to the details of the salvage. The President, fearing worldwide panic, ordered the entire project, 'Top Secret.' To keep people from spreading leaks of the project, he directed and organized a group of military officers to study the recovered ship and dead aliens, and then report to him. This group was labeled a 'black bag.' Which means, the members and directors within the group were eliminated from any and all records. This was to protect the entire project's secrecy from everyone, including high ranking military officers, and congressmen.

"They created a secret military base in the Nevada desert and called it 'S-1.' Today, the military base has moved slightly, and is called, 'S-4.' The people who ran the project were so serious about protecting it's secrecy, anyone suspected of leaking word of the base, was immediately killed. In order to get funding for the expensive base, the President initiated a funding program that would allow congress to annually pass cash into various 'black bags,' without ever knowing what the money was being spent on. It was argued that these kinds of projects are so secretive that their details could not be released to even the government. In fact, after the President's death, it was decided that this project not be disclosed to future presidents.

"Soon after the 1947 crash, the aliens were caught in a dilemma. They didn't want their presence known to anyone on Earth, yet the U.S. Government now knew of their presence. The aliens were afraid that the incident could ruin 90,000 years of work. So they did something dramatic. They struck a deal with the United States. The deal has come to be known as, 'The Dreamland Alliance.'

"Several nights after the accident, an alien ship landed right in the middle of an Air Force base where the ship was being kept. The aliens explained the basic premise of Devout Reality to a General, while also explaining the importance of keeping the alien project secret from the public. The aliens explained that abductions of various humans was going on, necessary, and completely safe.

"The General realized that he had a bonanza on his hands. World military tensions were escalating, and the U.S. was in need of technology they knew the aliens could provide. So the President, along with the General, devised a deal to exchange alien technology for the government's promise to keep the aliens' presence a secret from the public. Of course, the aliens didn't like this prospect. However, they sort of guessed that this was going to be part of a deal. So, instead they offered an exchange of computer technologies once every ten years, starting in the year 1953.

Every ten years, an alien delegate would meet at an Air Force base, and disclose to black bag members, limited computer technologies. The offer was agreed upon. The aliens knew that some of the technology would be used to develop weapons; however, so could all other technologies the U.S. government was interested in. Plus, computer technology, released every ten years, could increase worldwide communication. Which, of course, is a very important aspect of Devout Reality."

"So, some people on Earth know," Franky said amazed at what Emily told him.

"Well, sort of," she replied. "Today, not even the President of the United States knows of the alliance. Only a few members of the black bag know of the deal. They are the ones who every ten years prepare for the meeting, and take the technology given. The meetings are always held on December 23rd. So far, there have been three such meetings, in 1953, 1963, and 1973. The next one will be on December 23rd, in the year 1983."

"So, I guess if I remember everything, I would really mess things up, huh?"

"Now you understand," Emily said with a smile. "I hate to go into all that stuff with students, but sometimes it makes it easier for the student to understand why they must forget what they learn on a conscious level."

"Em, how many people have been taken here - to Fathom Sound?"

"Too many to count. But I'll tell you this much, you're in good company. Thomas Jefferson, Albert Einstein, Socrates, Homer, and Pericles were all abducted as children," Emily said as she stepped away from the cliff. "Come on, it's getting late and you haven't eaten dinner yet."

Emily and Franky arrived back to his room where dinner

was waiting. They ate, and reviewed the day's lessons. Soon, Emily said it was time to sleep. And again, as she left, he quickly fell asleep.

Suddenly, Franky was on the ground. The shock of hitting the ground woke him up from his sound sleep. He thought he must have rolled out of bed. The darkness of the room told him that it was still in the middle of the night. He stood back up and reached for the bed, and balanced himself. A noise outside peaked his interest as he froze so that he could hear better. It was a soft shuffling noise in the distance, so he quietly felt his way toward the window. Slowly lifting the cloth that covered the window, he could see a brilliant light rotating down on the beach. He could also see several students being led by their instructors toward the light. As he looked more closely at the various students, it appeared to him that they were in some sort of trance. They all seemed to be zombies to him. Franky's heart dropped as the door behind him suddenly opened. Franky tried to turn around, but blacked out.

The sun had just peaked above the horizon when Franky awoke. "Was that just another dream that I had last night?" he wondered aloud.

Chapter Four

The Shapes That Shadows Cast

"Let chaos storm!
Let cloud shapes swarm!
I wait for form."

-Robert Frost

October 18, 1976.
6:30 a.m.

Franky peaked out the window, and as he looked across the quiet village, he thought about his apparent dream from the previous night. He wondered where the instructors were taking all the students in the middle of the night. He also wondered about the bright light on the beach, and about his black out. But, what he really wanted to know was whether or not it was truly only a dream.

He was also extremely tired. Like all the mornings when he awoke at Fathom Sound, he was exhausted. However, this time he felt like he had not slept at all.

It wasn't long before Franky spotted the first instructors coming up the trail from the direction of the beach. Emily and Nathan walked together as they approached the village. Franky quickly sat down on the bed just as Emily knocked on the door.

"Come in!" he yelled. "I woke up early today," he said as Emily pushed open the door.

"I see that," she said with a serious look. "Are you ready?"

"Yup," he said while putting on his sneakers.

"We're going to meet Troy and his instructor, Nathan, on the beach," she said as they exited Franky's shack.

"He's going?"

"Nathan told me that Troy was excited about going to a city, and so he was happy to go along with the idea."

Halfway down the path to the beach Franky stopped and turned to Emily, "Em, where do you sleep?"

"All the instructors sleep on the other side of the mountain," she said pointing up to it. "That's not where we live, it's just where we sleep during the week of instruction. We all live in a city called Atlantis, and it's on a planet very far from here," Emily continued as she began to lead Franky again toward the beach.

"How do you get on the other side of the mountain?" he asked.

"Well, sometimes we all hike it together. It only takes about an hour or so. And sometimes, we take a helicopter ride over," she answered as they arrived on the beach.

One helicopter was already sitting on the beach with the engine off. Franky could see that Nathan was standing next to the pilot. Together, they approached Nathan.

"Good morning, Franky," Nathan said.

"Before Franky could reply, Troy stuck his head out of the cockpit of the helicopter, "Hey Franky, come here, you gotta check this out!"

Franky walked over to Troy and looked in. The pilot was human. His short brown hair gave him a typical military look. "Welcome aboard," the pilot said to Franky. "My name is Murray. You can call me Ray," he said extending his right hand out to Franky.

"My name is Franky," he said as he shook Ray's hand.

"Troy, now centered between Ray and Franky, separated the handshake with an outburst, "Is this week the first time that you've ever been up in a helicopter, Franky?"

"Yeah."

"This is an airspeed indicator. It tells you how fast the

helicopter is moving through the air - you know, sort of like a speedometer," Troy said pointing at a gauge. "And this is an artificial horizon. It tells you if you're flying straight. This one tells you how far above the sea level you are. It's called an altimeter."

Franky interrupted, "How do you know so much about flying?"

"I told you, my dad has to fly all the time, and I get to go a lot. So my dad gets some of the Air Force pilots to show me how to fly. Just basics. I told Ray if he needed any help, he could just ask me."

Emily and Nathan walked up behind them, "Come on guys, lets get in the back," Emily said breaking up the conversation.

Nathan, Emily, Troy, and Franky loaded into the back of the helicopter. The craft was the same type that brought them to the island. As they fastened their seat belts, the engine began to whine, and the blades above started to slowly spin. Soon the helicopter had lifted off the ground, and as the morning sun glared into the water next to Franky, he strained to look out over the ocean toward Memphis.

"How long will it take?" Troy asked.

"Not long. Twenty minutes maybe," Nathan replied.

Fifteen minutes passed, and as the mainland came into view, so did Memphis. Even though Memphis was still quite a distance away, Franky could tell that the largest building was in the shape of a pyramid, and it was located in the center of the city. Franky thought that the pyramid was much too large to be the one he saw in his dream.

The craft passed over the mainland beach and several fields came into view. Some of the them had strange shapes 'drawn' into the vegetation. Franky grabbed Emily's hand

and pulled her to the window. "What are they?" he asked.

"They're another example of how nature acts around a well ordered Social Order," she replied.

"You mean nature draws pictures in the fields around well ordered Social Orders?" he asked as he carefully studied each image displayed in the fields below.

"Well, kind of. As crafts like helicopters land, the vegetation may also react like that, if the occupants are from a magnitude nine Social Order," Emily clarified.

Suddenly, the helicopter began its descent. After landing in a field, the four departed the craft and began walking off in the direction of Memphis. They came up over a small hill and the outer rim of the city appeared before them. The first line of buildings were made of white glittering stone, and stood about 100 feet tall. Each building was identical, and rectangular in shape. The walls tapered off into a smooth curved roof. A foot bridge, crossing over a small river of crystal blue water, separated them from the city's entrance.

Franky noticed that the water didn't have any ripples so he took a step over to the waters edge and bent down. Carefully, he dipped his hand into the incredibly still water. His hand sank below the cool surface, but amazingly did not cause any wake. Franky jerked his hand in an effort to cause a splash. But again, he couldn't see any waves. Franky then lifted his hand out of the water and was again amazed as he noticed that his hand was not wet.

"What kind of water is this?" he asked as he attempted to cup some in his hands.

Emily grinned as she bent down besides him, "It's normal water. It's just acting differently around here."

Franky studied the water that he cupped in his hands. He rocked his hands back and forth, but still couldn't get the water to splash. Finally, he dumped the hand full of water over his head. It felt cool, like the water he was used to, as it ran down his neck. But, then it gathered together in the dirt at his feet, and streamed back into the brook, leaving Franky's hair and body completely dry.

"Come on," Emily said to Franky as she stood back up.

They crossed the foot bridge and stepped onto a cobblestone road. In the distance, the towering pyramid dwarfed any structure surrounding it.

"People live in these buildings?" Troy asked while pointing at the stone structures.

Nathan and Emily chuckled. "Not anymore," Nathan said. "It's hard to explain where they live. It's not a place I can show you, because it's not a place, it's not a location in time and space." Nathan could see the confusion on Franky's and Troy's faces. "One day, you'll understand."

Emily turned to the boys, "Now I want you both to stay next to us. If you want to see anything, just say so and we'll take a look. The people here are quiet people, we don't want to interrupt things, okay?"

"All right," the boys said in unison.

The group approached the city. The figure of a man standing next to a building came into view. The four approached, and as they neared him, he took a few steps to close the gap.

"Welcome to Memphis," he said without moving his lips.

Franky and Troy looked at each other bewildered.

"It's alright boys, he can speak to you in your minds. And you can speak to him just by thinking a thought," Nathan quickly said.

"My name is Odayus. I will be your guide through our beautiful city," he said.

"Odayus, this is Franky and Troy. They are students

from Fathom Sound," Emily said.

Odayus smiled. Dressed in a loose fitting rust colored robe, he removed its hood from his head. "I will speak aloud," he said as he bowed and gestured the group onward into the city.

"Our city, like nearly all cities on this planet, are circular in shape. A series of canals separate rings of land where our buildings rest. When you progress toward the center of these cities, you will find that the buildings become civic in nature. Instead of being resident dwellings, they become museums, restaurants, or what you would call science buildings," Odayus said as they walked past the first line of buildings.

"What's in that big pyramid?" Franky asked.

"You shall see, my friend," Odayus said.

As they crossed another bridge, many other residents of the city could be seen walking about. Some carrying baskets, others entering or exiting the first line of buildings. One odd thing that both Troy and Franky noticed was that there was very little noise. It seemed that the residents communicated telepathically, therefore the need for verbal conversation was obsolete. There was no sign of motorized modes of transportation, so that explained another good reason for the quiet. The group progressed through several rings of land, having to cross a bridge to access each strip of land. The further they progressed, the more curved the land looked. The pyramid at the center of the city now loomed only a few hundred yards away.

Franky and Troy gasped at the pyramid's size. They, however, gasped at something they found to be even more unbelievable. The pyramid did not come in contact with the ground! Hovering 100 feet above a pool of water at the geographic center of the city, the golden colored pyramid rotated slowly. A very slight hum could be detected only if everyone stood motionless, and the listener held his or her breathe and concentrated.

"What is it?" Troy asked.

Odayus slowly turned to the young boy with a smile. "It is a clock that predicts when nature will no longer be unpredictable."

Troy and Franky looked at each other confused.

Nathan jumped in, "This pyramid is thousands and thousands of years old. It is a relic to this city. Its exterior use is no longer needed here, but it remains unchanged. It is sort of like an antique."

"Oh, my mom has some of those. They're like really old things," Troy said.

"Yes," Odayus said. "Now sit," he continued as he pointed toward a set of benches. The four quickly sat down. "The wind here blows the pyramid around into a rotation. Clouds above take on a shape that is alike to the base of the great structure now before you. As they pass above, their shadows cast their image onto the ground. Then, only three times a day do the conditions exist where a cloud eclipses the sun at such an angle where the pyramid completely hides in the shadow of the sun. If the eclipse is perfect, the clouds shadow dimensions will perfectly match that of the pyramid. And if this perfection is met three times during the day, once at 25% through the daylight hours, once at 50% through the daylight hours, and once at 75% through the daylight hours, then all the Social Orders on Dreamland are perfectly well ordered. In a few moments, you will witness today's first eclipse!" Odayus said as he walked toward the great structure which stood nearly 2000 feet high.

Slowly the giant pyramid's rotation came to a stop, and

the winds about calmed to a point where they were no longer detectable. A great square shadow crept along below a cloud above. It slid across the water and began to cover the pyramid. And as the shadow slid up and over the structure, Odayus raised up his arms and cried, "Behold, nature shaped by consciousness!"

The shadow then perfectly covered the pyramid. As it did so, the surface of the structure began to glow golden white. Suddenly the great structure began to lower to the water surface. A door at the base of the pyramid suddenly appeared as a walkway materialized over the water leading up to the doorway. Odayus turned to the group, "Shall we enter?"

Amazed, Troy and Franky followed Emily's and Nathan's lead onto the walkway. When they entered the structure it became obvious that they were not the only people inside. The base of the structure was one large room were thousands of citizens walked about. Clear tubes of a bubbling fluid extended from the floor to the ceiling, which was about 100 feet high. The tubes were about 200 feet apart from each other. Many of the citizens simply sat next to each tube. Off to each side of the pyramid rose a stairway.

"What are all these people doing?" Franky asked as he pulled on the sleeve to Emily's robe.

"Um, I think their keeping their babies company," she responded.

"Yes!" Odayus said as he turned to Franky. "She said babies. Inside each tube is an infant that will one day be born and become a member to our society. The parents spend as much time next to each growing infant, talking at times to the infant telepathically."

"Why?" Franky asked. "I mean, I don't understand.

How do you have a baby if it's in a tube?"

Nathan took a quick look at Emily. "Be careful with this one," he whispered to her.

Emily looked down at Troy and Franky, "Well, each baby in a tube is a twin. Ah, a perfect twin of another baby that is not on this planet. All citizens of Memphis are people who have a twin brother or sister on another planet. So while one baby grows inside the stomach of a the mother on another planet, the twin of that baby grows inside one of these tubes next to an adoptive parent."

Nathan quickly walked over to a stairway, "Come on!" he called.

Troy and Franky followed Emily and Odayus toward Nathan. Franky thought the baby story very strange, and wondered if Emily was holding the whole truth back. The fact that there were pyramids on this planet, and he had dreamed about pyramids before actually seeing one, led him to believe that his dreams were fact. This made him wonder about the night before's dream, when he saw several students being led by their instructors toward a bright light on the beach. One student, he was sure he saw, was Emmanuel.

"Troy," Franky whispered as they started up the stairs, "I saw Emmaneul in the middle of the night being led toward the beach by his instructor."

"So. Maybe they were going to look at the stars or something." he said.

"Shhhh," Franky warned, "No! You don't understand. He was one of many students being taken down to the beach. And all of the students seemed, like asleep or something. Like they didn't know what was happening."

"Were their eyes open?" Troy asked.

"Yeah. I don't mean really asleep. I mean like

hypnotized or something," Franky tried to explain.

"You were probably asleep dreaming. Don't worry, I've had some weird dreams myself the last couple of nights," Troy responded.

Franky grabbed Troy's arm and stopped him, "Like dreams of a pyramid, not like this one, one that is white, and has the polis symbol above a doorway?"

"Yeah! But how did you kn. . ." Troy asked stunned.

"And did you dream about thousands of animals marching in straight lines across a desert?" Franky continued.

Troy could only shake his head, "yes."

"Come on you two!" yelled Emily. "It's lunch time, aren't you two hungry?"

Franky and Troy looked up at them and preceded again up the stairs until they reached the next level. A hallway led down into a cafeteria. A variety of food was offered, however, again meat was not available. "I could go for some pizza," Troy said.

"I think we can handle that," Odayus said as he signaled a man setting up a table of food. And within a few moments, they were seated at a table next to a wall, and a pizza was delivered to Troy and Franky. The wall by which they sat began to shimmer. Franky and Troy looked up to it, as it transformed into a window. They now had a wonderful view of Memphis. The pyramid was in motion once again, as Memphis appeared to spin below them.

"Oh neat! The pyramid is floating again!" Troy exclaimed.

"Yes. And it is being spun by the winds," Nathan added.

"What's it called? The pyramid. Does it have a name?" Franky asked looking at Nathan.

"All pyramids of this type are referred to as 'A Clock of

the Consciousness'," Nathan answered.

Just then a man wearing a blue robe stood up behind Nathan. The man glanced over at Odayus momentarily. On the man's face was a large discolored scar.

"What happened to that man?" Franky asked as he pointed to the man. "I thought things were perfect here. Can't you fix scars?"

"We put that scar on his face," Odayus quickly responded.

"What!?" Franky yelled.

"What Odayus means is, the scar is put there so that his twin on the other planet stays looking exactly alike," Nathan said.

"Why is looking exactly alike so important?" Franky asked.

"Since they are identical, they may mentally switch places one day. It's very difficult to explain, and I'm not sure why you ask," Nathan responded. Franky took that last comment as a cue to calm his questions. He also suspected that he struck a nerve.

After lunch, they preceded back down the stairway. Franky took some close looks at the tubes containing the babies. In the center of a blue tinted and bubbling water, floated a small red and flesh colored mass in the size and shape of a child's fist. A large black dot appeared at one end of the mass. This appeared to be one of the babies eyes.

After taking some more time around the room, Odayus said it was time to exit. They exited the pyramid in time to see the days final sun eclipse by a cloud. It was during these eclipses that the pyramid stopped rotating, and allowed entrance or exit of the massive structure. After exiting they preceded in the direction in which they entered the city.

"Odayus. Why make the building in the shape of a pyramid?" Franky asked.

"If it were any other shape, the shadow of the cloud would not perfectly, and completely cover every inch of its surface at the same time. The angled walls allow the shadow of a cloud that is not directly over head to blanket the pyramid," Odayus said without looking at Franky.

They reached the final bridge separating the city from the forest, and Odayus turned to the group and said, "Good bye."

The helicopter ride home was a quiet one. Franky was deep in thought. He was back to thinking that he must find a way to remember the lessons taught to him. Despite Emily's wishes, Franky was now determined to find a way to remember. The helicopter arrived back on Fathom Sound in time for dinner.

Dinner was to be held on the beach. Franky thought this might be a good opportunity to seek out Emmanuel. It didn't take long to find him. Troy and Franky quickly sat next to him.

"Oh hi, Troy!" Emmanuel said. "Hey," he said waving to Franky.

"Emmanuel, we got something to ask you," Troy said lowering his voice.

Franky leaned forward, "Emmanuel, last night, did your instructor take you down to the beach in the middle of the night?"

"In the middle of the night?" he yelled.

"Shhhhhh!" Troy and Franky whispered in his ear.

"Why don't you just broadcast our conversation?" Troy said sarcastically.

"No. I don't know what you guys are talking about,"

Emmanuel said annoyed.

Franky then caught Nathan staring at their meeting from across the beach. "Well, that's all we needed to know, see ya!" Franky said.

"But, he said. . ." Troy started.

"He said plenty! Lets go!" Franky said with his jaw clinched.

They ate dinner and returned to their rooms. Franky was determined to stay awake, but could not. In fact, by the next morning he couldn't even remember climbing into the bed.

Chapter Five

Recall Apex Of Fathom Sound

"Forgetfulness transforms every occurrence into a non-occurrance."

-Plutarch

October 19, 1976.
4:00 p.m.

℧he last five days seemed more like five weeks to Franky. So much swirled in his head as he sat back in his chair. Emily concluded her review of all the weeks' lessons. She reminded him that this was the last day, and that when he awoke tomorrow, he would be home, with no conscious memory of this incredible journey.

Franky was indeed a believer now. This is not to say that he had no questions. Emily told Franky to relax for a while and compose a few good questions. Franky decided that the best place for that was the beach, so he took a walk down the familiar trail. This free time was somewhat rare. Usually, by the time Emily concluded her lessons, night had arrived and it was time for sleep. If there was one thing Franky promised himself, it was to see that beach again.

As he walked down the sloping trail he could see several people on the beach, some sitting, some standing, most talking. Nearest to him was a group of ten sitting. At the opposite side was Nathan, and next to him was Troy.

When Franky approached the group, Nathan glanced up at him while continuing to address the group. Then Nathan paused, "Franky. Welcome. We were just going over some questions that the students have. Have a seat." The various members of the group gestured a greeting, while Troy indicated a space of beach next to him for Franky to sit.

Franky did so.

Nathan continued, "Lets see, where was I? Oh, let me tell you a little story. When I first arrived on this island, no one could swim in the water. There was a nasty little fish called a galatinsite. This little fish would give you a painful sting if you brushed up against it. The problem was that there was so many of them in close to the beach that you would have to be crazy to take a swim. Then, one day, a student threw some of her salad into the water after dinner. She wasn't littering. She just was trying to feed the fish. Well, wouldn't you know it, but a fish, called a blith fish, actually ate his radishes! So this young girl told her mentor, me. I was so happy that she made an effort not to waste her salad, but to share it by giving some to the fish, that I suggested that everyone feed the remainder of the radishes to the fish. The next night everyone threw radishes into the water. Much of the food was actually eaten by the bilth fish. We did this as a regular routine, and soon, the bilth fish multiplied in number just off our beaches. Well, it just so happens that this type of fish is a natural predator of the galatinsite. Over a few years, the blith fish population was so large, that the galatinsite were driven from our beaches. We no longer have the stinging fish on our beaches. So to speak, we gave to the fish, and the fish gave to us!"

"Now, don't get me wrong," Nathan quickly pointed out, "the Natural Order does not always work in such obvious ways, especially in climates that are not so close to a well ordered Social Order, but sometimes the Nature Order does come to one's aid in such an obvious way."

Nathan paused, then continued, "But I have to tell you all, this week was a waste if none of you go home and practice what we have taught you. It's going to be very hard at times, but no one expects any of you to be true Devout Realist, especially living on Earth in your era."

Troy interrupted, "Everyone's goal is to make money, I mean EVERYONE! And when you're living in that climate, how do you avoid greed, or envy?"

Nathan looked over at Troy, "Like I said, it's not going to be easy, but for the good of society, you must try to give at every opportunity."

"This is what I have trouble understanding," Franky said becoming noticeably tense, "You guys spend all this time with all these lessons, five days we've been here, and then tonight you're going to send us home with no memory? I mean, you're right! It's going to be hard living Devoutism on Earth, especially when you don't even remember the lessons you're taught. Why can't we just remember our stay here?"

Nathan sat patiently then answered, "Franky, we've been through this before. Remembering would cause complicated logistical problems. First of all, people would view these abductions and teachings as 'forced'. Then, imagine the panic if the general public thought that aliens were abducting their children. Besides, all of you will remember these lessons. As your grow older on Earth, and as you learn in school, slowly all of the things learned here will come to you. This is stuff that all of you were told about the first day you all arrived here."

Franky added to his question, "Well then, why do we just stay five days? Why not six or seven? There is so much more I think I need to know."

Nathan, for the first time, seemed to be annoyed by a question. He looked off into the sunset, and paused to gather a response. "Franky, that, for a lot of reasons, is not an easy question for me to answer. But, you asked a direct question, and I will answer it honestly. We have found that five days is the best length of time for a continuous stay. It has to do with memory retention. We call it the recall apex. You see, from the time you all arrived here, you have been bombarded with a sound frequency that you can not hear consciously. It is not harmful at all, but what it allows us to do is trace all the memories that you have of your stay.

"So as you learn something here, your brain is hearing this very high pitched sound. Thus, as these memories get stored in your brain, so does this very high pitched sound. That is how we can alter your memory. We will go after only the memories in your brain that have a trace of this very high pitched sound. Tonight, after you have fallen asleep, you will be treated by a type of magnetic field that will dislocate, NOT erase, all the memories tainted by these high pitched sound frequencies. Thereby dislocating your memories of Fathom Sound into your subconscious."

Franky's interest became noticeably peaked, "Does that mean since we got here on Fathom Sound, or does that include the mainland, and Memphis?"

There are transmitters near where we were on the mainland, and there are transmitters here on Fathom Sound. We had to install a temporary transmitter in Memphis just for yesterday. So, yes, that includes the mainland. However, the helicopter ride over may be a fuzzy spot for everyone. Although the trip to the island is well within the radius of the frequency waves, and since sound travels in straight lines, and the craft had some altitude, it is still possible that some of you may actually remember the helicopter ride as a dream. That is why we were careful what was said on the mainland," Nathan answered.

Someone in the group spoke out, "Is that why my animals go nuts some nights back on my farm? You guys are coming, making that sound like a dog calling whistle."

"Yes. In some cases that may be true. Some animals can audibly hear the frequency used. But in the cases that a dog may hear it on Earth, would involve the aliens themselves. The instructors are not used for abduction missions."

Franky interrupted, "So, right now we are being bombarded with those frequencies?"

"Yes, all the time while you are here." Nathan answered. "Franky, I think we should let someone else ask a question, don't you?"

"I'm sorry, I guess I got carried away," Franky said. But something Nathan had said spun the wheels in his head. He looked over at Troy sitting next to him and nudged him, as Nathan opened up the conversation to others in the group. Troy looked at Franky, as Franky jerked his head as if to suggest that they take a walk.

Franky and Troy got up, said their good-byes to the rest of the group, and walked down to the water's edge. As they neared the edge, Franky glanced around to insure that no one was near, and in a softened voice whispered to Troy, "I need you to come with me. I need your help, Troy."

Troy looked at Franky puzzled, and rebutted, "Help you? What are you talking about?"

Franky grabbed his arm and pulled him closer. "You want to remember everything about this place don't you?"

"Sure, but. . .," Troy was cut off by a persistent Franky.

"I think I know how! If our memories are being tainted, then all we have to do is make untainted memories!"

Troy looked at Franky with a frown, "And how are we supposed to do that, Einstein? Did you hear Nathan? He said those waves can travel far distances. And I haven't seen a car here, have you?"

Franky pulled Troy close again and smiled, "No, but, Nathan also said that sound travels in straight, line of sight, lines. That means they can't go through the ground!"

Troy again pulled back, "So what's that mean? We got to go around the world to get away from them. How's that going to help?"

Franky smiled and stood upright, his back to the island, as the sun set. The sun's rays now reaching the tops of the two peaks, reflected the last remaining light onto the beach. And with Troy's back to the ocean, this light caught his attention. It was right then that it hit him. The mountains. Franky smiling, knew by the look on Troy's face, that he understood Franky's intentions.

Troy took a step back. "Oh, no. I'm not going around no mountain, no way! Besides we would get caught and then be in trouble."

Franky stepped up to Troy, now nearing the ocean water. "Wait a minute, Troy, just listen. All we are going to do is just go around the mountain, make some memories that cannot be erased, and come back. No one will even know we were gone. Emily told me that it only takes about an hour to get there. Besides, what are they going to do, put us in detention?"

Troy finally lowered his voice, now knowing that Franky was very serious, "First of all, 'WE' are not going anywhere. Second of all, even if 'YOU' do go, your memories still might get erased, and that's if you don't get caught or hurt in the process."

Franky seemed to grow impatient. He knew that if he was going to try this stunt, he better slip off before everyone was ordered back to their rooms. "Okay, but Troy, do me just one favor. Walk down to the other end of the beach with me because it will not attract as much attention if we both casually walk together."

Troy nodded. "I can't believe you're going to do this! I'll walk down the beach with you. I think you're nuts, but I'll at least do that for you," he said, shaking his head nervously.

They walked about 100 yards away from the groups on the beach to where a group of trees separated the beach from the forest. Franky turned to Troy, with his heart pumping, and smiled, "Thanks."

Troy nodded again as Franky stepped off into the forest. Then Troy softly called, "Franky! Good luck, and if you remember me, look me up one day. I live in Sacramento!" Franky smiled, now fully in the woods, and said, "What was your last name again?"

"Bolger. Troy Bolger!"

"Okay. Troy Bolger, you got it!" And with that Franky turned and disappeared into the thick forest.

Franky felt panic rushing through his heart. A sense of urgency overwhelmed him. He ran through the forest as quickly as he could, although his speed was slowed by the darkness and thickness of an unfamiliar forest. His plan was to make a steady course inland and climb as high up on the first peak as he could. Then he would rotate around one side of the peak until he found himself on the other side. Once there he figured any frequency waves would be blocked by the mountains. Then, he figured, he could recall his stay at Fathom Sound, preserve his memories, and return quickly to the village.

At no point had Franky thought that he found a way to 'beat the system'. Instead, he took the perspective that he had nothing to lose. During the course of his stay, he was searching for a way to preserve his memories, and now he had a plan. Whether the plan was to work or not, he did not know.

As he jogged through the forest, its density seemed to lessen with every few minutes. Soon, the available light was increased by the vast array of stars from above as the tree cover lessened. The landscape here seemed more alien than back at the beach and village. At the village, many of the trees seemed to be Earth like. But here they were like no trees he had ever seen. They were white barked, very thin, and very tall. They were separated from each other by about twelve feet or so. As Franky hurried through, he could no help but think that the trees looked like white poles coming out of the ground. He also couldn't help wondering if his absence was noticed yet, as it had been a good twenty minutes or even maybe more since he had disappeared.

Tired, he could only half jog at this point, and he could tell by the increasing slope of the ground that he would need a reserve of energy as the hill became a mountain. Franky felt some guilt. He had been taught so much about honesty, truth, and virtue, and yet here he was running from those same mentors. But he justified this because he knew that if he could remember what he had been taught, then maybe he could teach what he had learned to the world once he returned. But he still couldn't fight the guilt. There were so many questions running through his mind. Despite what all the instructors said, he had some fears that there was still the possibility that the aliens intentions were not so civil. It was this confusion that drove him to this point, and it was the continued confusion that kept him running.

He continued his off and on again run up the slope of the sparsely treed mountain. As he did, the temperature steadily decreased. Now and then, Franky could see the snow capped peak. So when he came to a small clearing, he stopped. He turned around and looked down the mountain.

He could see the water off in the distance reflecting the stars. Above he could clearly see the peak. Franky determined that he was about half way up the mountain, and since the slope was becoming steeper, he decided to begin the trip around the mountain to the right. Then before he could begin to run, he felt a presence. His heart raced faster as he stopped again. He looked back in the direction of the village. Then a flash caught his attention above him. He looked up to see two stars moving around each other. They almost seemed to dance. Suddenly they fell straight down toward the island. They streaked down in the vicinity of the village, then came to a sudden stop directly over the village. They hovered there for a few moments then vanished. Franky wondered if that could be a sign that his disappearance was noticed.

"Were they aliens?" he wondered. In either case, he now felt more pressed than ever before to get around the mountain. Fear fueled him as he darted off along the side of the mountain.

A half an hour passed before Franky began to notice a light coming from around the side of the mountain that he was approaching. Much of the tree line was below him by this point, so he headed for some trees just below him. It appeared as though he could move along the tree line toward this brilliant light. Its rays shot straight out from the place Franky planned to go; directly between both peaks.

Out of breath and out of energy, Franky slowed to a walk as he approached the light. As he neared a ridge, he could tell that he would be able to see its source once he looked over the ridge. Once he climbed near the top of the ridge, he stopped and peered down into the light and valley between the peaks.

"Was this where Emily sleeps?" he wondered. The light was glowing out of the air in the form of a giant ring surrounding the entire valley. There were no light fixtures, the light just seemed to beam right out of thin air. On the valley itself, Franky could see thousands of twinkling lights. He thought the twinkling lights were houses. "This is where she sleeps," he said to himself.

Directly below him was a stone platform adjacent to a white pyramid. It was the pyramid Franky saw in his dreams. Above a door way, was the polis symbol. There was no doubt about it, this was the same pyramid. Franky knew that he was here before. Around the pyramid, parked on the stone platform, were ten helicopters. The same ones that he had flown in.

Franky slowly maneuvered into the trees on the other side of the ridge. Not knowing if he would be seen, he made sure to stay under the cover of trees while he made the descent down the mountain toward the structure. Then suddenly, he stopped. Franky realized that he made it to the other side of the mountain.

Franky sat down and began running through the entire stay at Fathom Sound in his head. He remembered the laws of nature, society, and that of the universe. He remembered Memphis, Odayus, Emily, Nathan, and of course Troy Bolger from Sacramento. After he felt comfortable with his recall, he continued down the mountain. He only hoped that no frequencies were being generated from the facility that he approached.

As he closed the distance, Franky heard a sudden hum ahead. Stopping to take a better listen, he heard the hum grow louder. Quickly, he ducked into some surrounding brush. Franky immediately recognized the sound as an approaching helicopter. The trees around him whipped wildly as the thundering craft passed above him. Landing next to the pyramid, Franky was shocked to see several dazed looking students unloading out of the helicopter. Guided by their instructors, each student entered the pyramid.

After about fifteen minutes, the students returned to the helicopter still appearing to be dazed. The helicopter quickly lifted off the platform and departed back in the direction of the village. "Maybe no one noticed that I'm gone," he wondered. He figured he had a little extra time, so he ran across the platform, and up to the pyramid door way. After looking around to insure that he was not spotted, he entered the pyramid.

This pyramid was tiny compared to the one in Memphis. Its height was not much higher than 100 feet. As he entered the small dwelling, a soft light lit the four inward slanting walls. Franky looked for the source of the light, but could not find one. Suddenly the corners to each wall became a blur. As Franky focused, he realized that he could no longer see the floor, walls, ceiling or the door that he used to enter. It seemed as though he was now floating in a thick fog. Then seeping through fog came a hint of images to come in the form of swirling colors.

Rising above a dry plain with no noticeable acceleration, Franky was somehow transported to another place. Across this plain a thunderous roar off in one direction caught his attention. Quickly, he was thrust higher into the sky. On the horizon, a plume of smoke filtered into the air. The smoke was not from a fire. It was a cloud of dust. From across the desert the stampeding creatures came once again.

Hanging above that stampede, the art of chance folded below him. The beasts had been running in columns, all parallel to one another. "This must be a spin off of a well ordered Social Order nearby!" he deducted. The creatures were indeed progressing in symmetric from, so could they have somehow been interacting with the Natural Order? Was he watching the physics of Devout Reality take hold of nature, like it does to the clouds? "The Social Order nearby must be a nine," he thought. "This is a new lesson, or is it?" he wondered. Franky's memory became twisted. "I've seen these animals before", he said to himself, "Where am I?" he wondered. "I'm in the pyramid still! I want out!" he screamed as he suddenly remembered how he got to the desert plain.

Instantly the images disappeared, and the doorway materialized. Franky rushed outside. He caught his breath while he leaned against the pyramid walls. Everything began to come back to him - where he was, how he got there. Then the purpose of the pyramid dawned on him. "It's some kind of teaching machine!" he said aloud to himself. "The images seen in the pyramid will be remembered by the students, even consciously, because the mountain blocks the sound frequencies that erase memories!" he thought. Then another fear struck him. He wondered how long he had been gone from the village. "Maybe they were going to leave without me!" he feared. "Maybe they never realized that I was gone!" Not knowing how much time he had, Franky quickly turned back toward the village. His objective complete, he wanted to get back to the village.

As he reached the ridge and raced back into the darkness of the mountain, the beach and the village came into distant view. He could see aerial activity. Lights and movement were very obvious. Then, three lights that were hovering above the village, suddenly separated from each other and shot out in different directions across the tops of the trees, with one rapidly coming toward Franky. Franky knew that these were not helicopters because of their speed and instant acceleration. He feared that due to his absence, the aliens might have been summoned somehow. "Maybe the aliens organized a search," he thought as he continued to race down the mountain into the trees in the direction of the village. His heart was pounding hard, as he navigated through the tall white thin trees.

Then, as if in slow motion, a light beam from above caught him in the trees as he ran. Franky froze, and turned to see the craft hover silently closer to him. A red glowing ball flared out from the bottom of the vessel and engulfed him, causing him to fall to the forest floor unconscious.

Chapter Six

Perspectives

"They (aliens) alter consciousness and affect people's anticipatory powers. They modify visual perceptions so that people have difficulty seeing objects close to them or discerning spatial relationships well. They interfere with people's volition and force them to do things against their will - and do this from afar. They mitigate fear and stop physical pain. They institute selective amnesia, communicate telepathically, and create complex images in peoples minds."

-Dr. David M. Jacobs
"Secret Life"

October 19, 1976.
Approximately 11:00 p.m.

He was frozen in fear. Franky could hear his head vibrate against a cold table as he trembled. Then the sound of feet shuffling across the floor startled him further. Afraid to open his eyes, he pretended to stay asleep. It was coming back to him now. The red flare had struck him, and now he laid on a hard surface in a very quiet setting. Franky could tell that there was a very bright light in this room, as its glare attempted to squeeze between his eyelids.

Something brushed up against his leg. Franky decided to take a peak. Slowly he open one eye. Standing over him, and staring back at him was what he feared. A white skinny creature with large dark eyes had not been taken off guard by Franky's attempt to take a peak. Startled, Franky opened both eyes wide, and sat quickly up off the table.

"Don't hurt me!" he cried as he slide off the other side of the table and held his hands up in a self defensive posture.

The creature stood about five feet tall. Humanoid in shape, however very thin. The creatures waist seemed no wider than an adult human males leg. Its mouth was nothing more than a small slit; no lips. Its head was unproportionally large, and had no visible ears, eyebrows, or hair. Its nose was barely visible.

Alerted by the sudden noise, two more aliens entered the

bright white room from one side. They gathered on the other side of the table from Franky. One glanced at the other, suggesting non-verbal communication was taking place.

"I'm sorry! I won't ever do anything like that again! Please don't hurt me!" Franky pleaded.

The creature in the center raised one of its hands slowly toward Franky. And as it did, much of the fear Franky was feeling dissolved from his emotions. "We are not going to harm you, Franky," one said through Franky's head. "Everything will be okay. Everything is fine. You are fine. There is no pain. You will go home," it continued.

Franky felt subdued. He stayed aware of the surroundings, and was alert, only his emotion of fear was lessened. Franky glanced around the room. Oval, he could not identify where the walls met the ceiling or floor. They all kind of blended together in a bright white milky color.

"Where am I?" he asked.

"You are on our ship, but you will be okay," they communicated.

"I'm going home?" Franky thought.

"Soon. First, we will need to take you to a hospital. There we can repair the damage done to your memory."

"Damage to my memory!" Franky thought. "You mean you want to erase my memories of Fathom Sound, don't you?"

The three aliens glanced at one another. Two of the creatures slipped out of the room. "Everything is okay," it assured. "Soon you will be home with your family and friends. Then you will be happy again. Everything will be the same as it was."

"I don't want it to be the same as it was! I want to remember!" Franky yelled verbally. "Why can't anybody see that? What is so hard to understand about that?"

The alien moved toward the exit. "Follow me," it commanded.

Franky had no intention of following anyone. But before he could think, he was already following the creature. Shocked, he looked down at his own disobeying legs, as they transported him down a hallway.

"You like airplanes," it communicated in Franky's head as it always did. "This is how we fly this craft," it said as they entered a black room.

Standing in the center of the room, Franky wheeled around and suddenly realized that the door entrance was gone. At that point, stars appeared all around both of them. It was as if they were floating in space without space suits. Franky looked down at his hand, and was shocked to see he was holding the aliens four fingered hand.

"Look forward, Franky. Think about going there," it commanded.

Franky looked forward and spotted a tiny star off in the distance. "Go there!" he said aloud.

"No. You can not say 'go there', you must think, 'go there'," the creature clarified.

Franky looked back at the tiny star and closed his eyes as he concentrated. He was about to say that it was no use, when he opened his eyes to find stars streaking by the two of them. The alien cracked what appeared to be a slight grin. The tiny star quickly became an orange ball of fire millions of miles across.

"Wow! I can do it!" Franky said excitedly. "If Troy only saw this cockpit. No altimeter, or airspeed indicator, or artificial horizon. Not even a steering wheel!" he thought.

The alien pointed to a star above their heads, "This one,"

it commanded.

Franky looked up at it, closed his eyes once again. And when he opened them he was again greeted with stars zipping by in a blur. The star, the alien pointed out, was soon before them. The alien seemed to take control, as the star flew close off to their left. Ahead a shiny star grew larger as it became obvious that it was really a planet.

A blue and white atmosphere made Franky wonder if this was really Earth.

"No. This is not Earth. This is where the hospital is. It is also where Emily lives," the creature communicated.

They rushed into the planet's atmosphere, then slowed suddenly. Like a train on a rail, they glided without sound into the white and blue atmosphere. On closer inspection, the atmosphere appeared orange and yellow toward the north. The black skies of space turned to deep purple, then blue, as clouds appeared below. They too were square in shape. They descended down to them effortlessly, then just above them, they glided through spaces between several clouds. "The alien was putting on a show for me," Franky thought.

Then suddenly the ship rolled hard right, Franky's feet stuck firm somehow, as they shot down inverted toward the now visible city below. It was nestled at the rim of a vast area of water, possibly an ocean. No signs of smog or pollution could be detected. The ground raced toward them, and without any deceleration, they stopped immediately above a structure of concrete or something that color. The building appeared many thousands of feet high. The top was much more narrow then the base, although this was not the familiar pyramid shape. There was a flat level section that made up the roof. Along the sides of the structure were thousands of rectangular openings where silvery disks entered and exited at each level.

The vessel slowly descended down the massive structure until it reach about the mid point. They then moved into one of the openings. Inside, was a huge dock like chamber with hundreds of those silvery disk crafts laying motionless on platforms. All of the vessels were oval, with very thin edges, but wide in the middle. They came quickly to a rest on a platform. A spot apparently had been reserved for them. The creature then made a slight hand movement, and the walls in front of Franky seemed to suddenly melt away to form a ramp leading off the ship and onto the platform. As they exited the ship, a gush of air flowed up from the platform floor. The wind pushed Franky's hair up into the air.

Franky stepped down onto the platform with the alien just behind him. Suddenly, hundreds of alien creatures came pouring out of one of the buildings large doorways. Franky quickly was surrounded by hundreds of aliens. The nearest ones reached out to touch him about his arms and head. By the way all of the creatures we reacting to Franky's presence, it must have been a rare thing for a human to be at that hospital. The commotion was so great that were not that fear was somehow dissolved from his emotions, Franky just might not have been able to take the dramatic scene without panicking.

They entered a hallway with no door. After passing through it, all sound and wind stopped. This seemed strange to him. The strong wind should have been forced through any hall that had no door. They walked down the hall in silence. Franky turned to look behind at the garage, and saw that the crowd stayed behind. Franky now followed the alien to their destination, wherever that would be.

They entered a large round room that had no visible

ceiling. A sudden turn to the right and the alien pointed to a wall. Like in the ship, the wall melted, revealing a room inside. Franky stepped inside to find a bed. He sat down, and when he looked up, the alien was gone and the doorway had quickly become the wall. Franky jumped up to the wall and began to probe it with his fingers. "Let me out!" he cried. "I am not a prisoner!"

After some time of useless attempts to open the wall, he sat back down on the bed. The room was the familiar sterile white. "They think I'm an animal," he thought. A tear rolled down his face. "I'm tired of this, I just want to go home. Okay?!" he screamed, "I just want to go home now! Take me home!" he yelled again as tears now flowed down his trembling face.

Then, fatigue hit him. "Sleep," he heard in his head. Fighting the powerful feeling to sleep proved useless, as his head hit the pillow provided for him.

Franky opened his eyes to a familiar room that surrounded him. The tall white walls extended up to the tinted windows that he remembered from a dream he had on Fathom Sound. Franky, laying on a table, quickly turned his head to his left where he saw his image, or was it an unknown twin brother laying next to him? A wire ran out the back of Franky's head, and into the wall behind him. Another wire then ran out of the wall and into the head of the image next to him. "It must be a mirror," he assured himself. They laid there starring at each other.

To Franky's horror, the image of himself laying next to him spoke! "Hello," he said.

Confused, Franky turned his head back and faced the tinted windows above, "Take me home!"

Chapter Seven

Real Mind Realities

"We are near awakening when we dream that we dream."

-Novalis
"Pollen"

October 21, 1976.
9:00 a.m.

F ranky woke with a powerful headache. He reached for his pounding head as he let out a moan.

"Need some aspirin?" a voice asked.

Franky froze. He opened his eyes to find himself laying on a sofa. Seated next to him was a woman with blond hair pulled back into a ponytail.

"Oh, my name is Emily," she said.

"Where am I," Franky asked as he looked up at Emily.

"I know that this is going to be hard to believe, but you're in a city called Atlantis," she replied.

"Who are you? I know you from somewhere," he said trying to sit up.

"Don't you need that aspirin?" she said as she stood up and walked out of the room. "Water okay?"

"Ah, yeah, I guess," he said still confused.

Emily quickly returned to the sofa and handed the aspirin to him with a glass container of water. "Thanks, Em," he said.

"Em?" he thought. "Okay, what's going on, where am I, and who are you?" he said now demanding an answer.

"As I told you, my name is Emily. You do know me. Over the past week, you and I have been studying a subject called Devout Reality. You learned very quickly and we had some fun over the last few days. But, something went wrong at the end of the five day trip. It involved your memory. So your memory of the last week has been completely removed. Now you have to relearn Devout Reality."

"Devout Reality? Where am I?" he asked as he looked around the room.

"Well this is the hard part. You see, Franky, this is not Earth that you are on. This is a planet that I live on," she said not sure how Franky would react.

But Franky reacted smoothly. What she did not realize was that at the moment she mentioned Fathom Sound, memories of the island flashed into his head. As time went by, slowly more and more memories surfaced. So Franky sat calmly and listened, knowing in some cases what she was about to say, before she said it.

Emily continued, "I will be your guide for the next few days," she said convinced that Franky did not remember Fathom Sound as he really did.

Franky played along by asking a question that he knew the answer to, "Are you from Earth, Emily?"

"Well, Franky, I was once on Earth, a very long time ago. But hardly anyone you meet here has ever see Earth. Almost everyone in this city, Atlantis, was born on this planet. Some of us are what you might call, 'test tube babies'. Nearly everyone here is a clone. Only very, very few of us were actually born on Earth like you, Franky.

"Clone?" Franky said unsure of what she meant.

"Uh, yes. Science can allow us to make a duplicate of another person or animal, or even a plant. The duplicate will be identical. More so than a twin. Even identical twins have some differences. Our clones have no differences."

"Are you a clone?" he asked.

"No. I don't even have a twin."

Emily went on to explain that he would be here for five days to learn about Devout Reality. She covered the entire agenda and answered some of Franky's immediate questions. All the while, Franky kept to himself that he completely remembered everything that occurred on Fathom Sound. His plan had apparently worked. Emily then started the first day's lessons. After dinner, she showed him to his room.

As he laid in his bed, he could not help but feel as if he had been in this house before. He seemed to know every little twist and turn of the walls. He even knew where to find a hair line crack in the window of his bedroom. He could only remember his room on Fathom Sound, so why was this house so familiar? He thought maybe he had been here, and the aliens were successful at removing that part of the brain. Secretly, Franky congratulated himself. His trip around the mountain on Fathom Sound seemed to have worked after all.

In the middle of the night, Franky awoke to loud voices coming from the living room area. Each of the voices was familiar. They were members of his family, his friends, school teachers, and Emily. They were all speaking at once, and all seemingly not in conversation with each other, just rambling on, and growing louder. Franky saw a strong light seeping into his bedroom from underneath his door, and as it did, fear swelled into him once again.

He looked to the window and quickly ran to it. He slid it open, and slipped into the night, leaving the voices behind. Upon his touching the ground, though, the black sky above filled up with a neon red light. And in front of him, in the bushes and trees, hundreds of eyes lit up, reflecting the red sky.

Franky ran from the back to the front yard. The sky

was still ablaze, as he continued to run onto a walkway that lead away from the house. The voices, though now not as loud, followed him. He ran across a small foot bridge that crossed a river. Everywhere he looked he saw no one. Just up ahead, he saw a home very familiar to him.

It was a rancher that looked exactly like the one he lived in on Earth. Tired, he released his final burst of energy to reach the front door. He did not notice someone sitting on the porch bench next to him as he attempted to open the front door.

"You're too late," a boy said dressed in a rust colored robe sitting on the porch bench.

Startled, Franky turned to look at him. A large hood covered the boy's face. "There's nobody home," the boy said.

"Who are you," Franky asked.

The boy stood while removing the hood, "My name is Franky. Franky Carter."

Franky's shock paralyzed him. His mouth dried as he looked into the face of what appeared to be an identical twin of himself.

The boy continued, "I've been expecting you, Franky. Don't be afraid. I know we look alike. That's because you are my clone."

"Wait, you mean you are MY clone, don't you?" Franky asked as his heart pounded in his throat.

"I don't have much time to explain. You'll just have to believe me. You are my clone, you live here, in Atlantis, you always have. Doesn't this town seem familiar? You live here, and I live on Earth. The lessons you learn will be transplanted to me one day. So you must remember everything. You must try not to forget, do you understand?" the clone asked as he put his hand on Franky's shoulder.

"No, not really," Franky replied.

"Just try to remember, you must remember," Franky heard as he suddenly found himself quickly sitting up out of his bed full of sweat. Franky looked around the room and notice the window was closed. "Another dream," he thought. But thus far, nearly all his dreams had some significance, and meaning. Franky remembered back to Memphis, how the citizens were growing thousands of babies in tubes. Could he have come from such a place? The instructors on Dreamland were said to be usually twins. Could they have meant clones? But why? "Why?" he wondered. Franky had enough. That morning he was going to get some answers from Emily.

October 22, 1976.
7:00 a.m.

Franky was waiting for Emily to wake. Sitting on the sofa he wondered how she would react. At this point, finding out the truth seemed more important. Emily was surprised to see Franky awake.

"Em, I think that there is more going on here than what you've told me," he said sternly.

Emily quickly took a seat on a chair. "Go on," she said sincerely.

"Do I have a twin brother?" he said swallowing hard and blushing.

Emily's distress showed immediately as she opened her mouth wide, "Ohhhh." After quickly regaining her composure she looked into his eyes. "I don't know where you got that, but you've kinda messed things up around here, Franky. Let's see. Franky, like most children your age, you are very curious, and well, let's just say that your particular curiosity has managed to cause some problems. So I'm going to be honest with you, but you must promise something," she said pausing with a demanding look in here eye. Emily also figured that it was likely that Franky remembered the events at Fathom Sound.

"What's that?" he asked.

"You have to obey the rules I set until the lessons are over. No running off into the woods, or going off on your own. You must return to Earth, exactly as scheduled! Deal?"

"Deal," he agreed, happy to learn that he was not going crazy.

"Some of the things I'm going to explain may be premature to your lessons, but in light of the circumstances, we will give it a shot and hope you understand everything. In a real sense, you do have a twin brother. His name is Franky. Before you were born, your genetic make-up was retrieved from your mother and father. You, and your 'twin' brother, were conceived in a "test-tube" so to speak, then your 'twin' was transplanted in your mother. You however, Franky, were born and raised here, in Atlantis."

"No!" Franky screamed as he leaped up off the sofa. "That's not true! It can't be true! I live on Earth! I live in New Jersey . . . I can name all my friends, all my teachers!" he yelled as he backed away from Emily while tears rolled down his face. "How can I be from both places?"

"Search within your heart, I know that you will find that what I am saying is the truth," she said approaching him calmly. "You live here, with me."

"How then could I know all those people on Earth? What are you saying, that my life never existed?" he said still crying.

"Not at all," Emily said in her typical calm voice. "Your memory has been tampered with by the aliens."

"Oh, great! That makes me feel a lot better!" he said shaking.

"Let me finish. One Franky lives on Earth, in New Jersey, and the other lives here in Atlantis. You are the Franky that lives here in Atlantis with me."

"But then why don't I remember you and Atlantis like I remember Earth?" he asked.

"Like I said, your memory has been altered. We want to teach children on Earth about Devout Reality. Bringing them to Fathom Sound for several days was the best way, but there are a lot of problems in transporting little children halfway across the universe."

"Like what? I mean you guys are like superman only much better. What can't you do?" he asked.

"There are problems with that kind of operation. First of all, if we bring anyone from Earth to another planet, and expose them to that planets environment they would die in hours. Any simple bacteria from another planet is so different from any on Earth that a human body that lived on Earth couldn't defend against it. And what about the five days. What are we supposed to do, leave a note on the children's pillows with a date of expected return stamped on it? And to top it off, how are we suppose to teach such complex subjects to 10 year old Earth boys and girls? They simply would not understand the subject matter."

"I am from Earth! This is a trick! Take me home!" he yelled as he pushed Emily away and ran into his bedroom. Franky slammed his door shut, and climbed under the bed crying.

Hours went by before Franky's sobbing dried. Emily figured that it was best that he spend some time alone, so she did not attempt to disturb him. As he climbed out from under the bed, he noticed that it was raining outside. He stepped to the window, and as he watched a rain drop snake down the glass pane, he remembered the hair line crack in the window that he saw the night before. "This house does seem so familiar," he thought. "Maybe Em is telling the truth." Franky walked to the bedroom door, slowly reached for the handle, and opened it. Franky saw that Emily was sitting quietly on the sofa, staring out the window, with tears of her own rolling down her face. Something about that scene hurt his feelings. Emily was more to him then an instructor, she was his mother. And right then and there he knew that.

"You mean, I'm smarter than the Earth Franky?" he said as he walked up to her slowly.

Emily smiled in relief and wiped her face with a towel. "You worried me there for a minute. I was saying to myself, 'See Em, see what honesty gets you!'."

"Look, you're not out of the woods yet! There are more questions," he said without cracking a smile.

"Okay, any question you have, I'll answer. Where was I?" she asked.

"You were saying how smart I am," he answered.

"And how modest too!" she added with a snicker. "We were talking about how difficult it is to bring Earth children across the universe for a week without anyone on Earth knowing it. The solution to all those logistical problems was simple. The aliens created clones. One was educated in an alien environment, while the other on Earth with their family. Now the alien clone's education is much more advanced, so intellectually, they are far superior to the Earth clone. Once the Earth clone reaches a certain maturity, the alien clone is brought to a hospital at his will.

There, his or her memory of his life is displaced so that he or she has sort of like amnesia. Then, the Earth clone is abducted and placed side by side in the alien ship. The Earth clone's memory is then downloaded into the alien clones brain."

"So like, my memories of Earth are really not my memories at all? They have just been planted there by the aliens?" he asked.

"Yes. That's right. Then the alien clone is taken to an island called Fathom Sound, on another planet, and Devout Reality is learned," she continued.

"The alien clone there thinks he's from Earth. But he's not. Right?" he asked.

"Exactly. That way the subject matter of Devout Reality can be learned by a ten year old without fearing virus infections, and we don't have to worry about children missing on Earth."

"But why not just download Devout Reality directly into abductee's heads?" he asked, "Or better yet, why not have the alien clone learn Devout Reality as himself, then download the lessons into the Earth clone?"

"Impossible. First of all, downloading is not so simple. It can only be done between two identical brains. Secondly, the Earth clone must learn Devout Reality using many of their own unique personalities and life experiences. Otherwise, the downloading may be rejected."

"So I'm the alien Franky," he said still finding it hard to believe and handle.

"Yes, you live right here with me. I raised you," she answered.

"So aliens abduct people on Earth without their knowledge?" he asked.

"Yes. Quite regularly. There are several different types

of abduction.   There is the 'Opportunistic Abduction'.
That's when aliens may come across an individual or
individuals in a deserted setting.   They are giving an
examination to determine whether or not they are suitable
for impregnation so that a clone can be generated, all for the
purpose of one day learning Devout Reality."

"So that's what happened to my - or I mean, the Earth
clone's parents, right?" he asked.

"Yes.   Then there is the 'Routine Abduction'.   This is
done at least once every year for the first 12 years of an
Earth clones childhood.   The child will be abducted for two
main reasons.   To insure that they are healthy, and to insure
that no scars or other physical differences have occurred.
If scars do exist, then the identical scar is created on the
alien clone."

"Why, I mean what for?" he asked.

"Well now, what do you think would happen if the Earth
clone looked down and noticed that his five inch leg scar
was gone while on Fathom Sound?   You know what would
happen."

"I didn't think of that," he said shaking his head.

"What about switching?" he asked.

"What?" she said unsure by what he meant.

"You know, switching.   Do alien and Earth clones ever
switch places?"

"No!   That's not done," she said harshly.

"So like, how do you know?   I mean, can you blindly
trust these aliens?" he asked.

"Yes. How much do you remember of Fathom Sound?"
she asked.

"Very little!" he said as he lied as best he could.

"I figured you remembered some," she said with a grin.

"Well, in case you don't remember, the basic acting

principle behind Devout Reality is - to give. How is that devious?"

"It's not. But abducting people without their consent, that seems wrong," he said slowly.

"What determines right and wrong?"

"To give is right," he answered.

"Right. That's what the aliens are doing by abducting. Giving knowledge that will benefit the society," she said quickly.

"I remember that you said that they live forever, is that true?"

"Everything I've told you about them is true. So yes, they live forever."

"Do you? I mean, will we live forever?" he asked.

"No. Not in this form anyhow. We will have a normal life span," she responded.

"Why can't we live forever? Is it impossible or something?" he asked confused.

"No. We too could live forever, if we underwent a complex genetic change. And this same genetic procedure in stopping the aging process has dramatic side effects. Complete hair loss is one of many. Our skin would lose its color, and its texture would become stiff. Cartilage in our ears and nose would also disintegrate over time. Now Franky, if I looked like that when you first saw me on Fathom Sound, how would you have felt? Not too comfortable, right?"

"Yeah, I guess. But what did you mean by saying, 'not in this form'?"

"Nothing ever really dies," she answered. "There is a cosmic consciousness that flows through all things in the universe. This consciousness is a timeless and spaceless state of awareness. Our individual consciousness may seem to be seperate from the cosmic consciousness, but it is not. Each person's brain and body chemistry interacting with the cosmic consciousness make up that person's own consciousness. Right now, your consciousness is the same as mine. But because your brain is different than mine, and you have different memories than I do, our consciousness takes on a very personal and different appearance. Take away our brains, and the two consciousness are the same. So when our bodies die, our consciousness will merge with the cosmic consciousness. By the way, this is how communication through the mind is possible. Since all things share the same consciousness, it is possible to communicate through it."

"But then why do the aliens live forever?" he asked.

"Well, it's hard to explain but, their home is the cosmic consciousness. They are able to leave their bodies and enter it at will."

"So that's why we all don't live forever. Our appearance would change, and because we would never enter the cosmic consciousness?" he asked.

"You sort of got it. The only thing is, we are always connected to the cosmic consciousness, it's just not plainly obvious. Plus, if you underwent the physical changes to prevent aging, you would no longer be identical to the Earth Franky, now would you?" she added.

"So, I would then have no purpose for living. . ." he said finishing what he thought she was about to suggest.

"I didn't say that. You have a wonderful life here in Atlantis. Remember, your memory has been displaced so that you learn as the Earth Franky would learn. Please don't assume too much about the Atlantis you. Look, I know that this is all very confusing to you, you're just going to have to trust me at this point. You, the Atlantis Franky, wanted to do this whole procedure. You were not forced into doing anything.

"The learning of Devout Reality is vital to humanity. It is the next social step of human consciousness, but it is also the hardest plateau to reach. In order to get there, human nature itself has to change. Those negative emotions like pride, greed, and vengeance must be reduced from human nature. The people in Memphis all had genetic alterations so that those emotions were reduced. Some of those genes have been spread in people on Earth already. The most exciting thing you have not heard yet, is that after so many years of effort, the day is near. Very near!" Emily said smiling.

"What kind of day?" he asked.

"The aliens have said that soon, the first Social Order on Earth will enter the positive spiral of the Natural Order, it will become a magnitude seven Social Order. If you remember, once a Social Order enters that upward spiral, there is no return. Eventually, that means that Social Order will become a magnitude nine Social Order - a Collective Inception."

"Collective Inception? What's that?"

"That's a term used to describe a magnitude nine Social Order."

"Oh. When is this day coming, and to what Social Order?" he asked.

"I don't know. But the aliens do. I do know that the Social Orders will be in North America, and Western Europe," she said as she stood up. "Follow me, I want to show you something out back."

Franky stood up and followed her out the back door. The rain had passed, leaving the ground and vegetation damp. They walked up a natural slope in the backyard that lead toward a wooded area.

Emily continued her discussion as they entered the woods, "Look around you, Franky. Do you see any one tree in this forest exactly alike?"

"Yeah, they all seem alike - and all evenly spaced apart," he said looking around.

"Now on Earth, as you know, trees in nature are never like this. They come in random sizes and at random distances from each other. That's because in nature, everything is in a state of disorder. Things just happen, for the good or bad. But here on this planet, it's just the opposite; nature is in a state of order. Nature only gets like it does around here, during a Collective Inception. Look at that field," she said pointing to a clearing. They stopped at the field's edge.

"Do you see that animal?" she said pointing to a cat sized creature crossing the field slowly.

"Ah, yeah, I see it."

"Good, now look over there. Do you see that tree?" she said pointing to a tree across the field.

"Yeah," he replied again.

"Just keep your eyes on that tree." And as she finished the sentence, a dark object seemed to fall from the tree, but just before hitting the ground, it rose abruptly back up off the ground about three feet and with amazing speed and stealth, zeroed in on the animal crossing the field. As it struck the creature with great power and speed, the two creatures tumbled in the grassy field. Franky could see the huge powerful jaws of the gliding creature clamped down on its prey.

"The creature that flew out of the tree is called a stampler. You see, Franky, the stampler didn't always fly. Through evolution, it developed that key ability. A long time ago, out of pure chance, a stampler was born with a deformity. It had a long flat ridge across it's head, almost like a hammerhead shark. And with the gravity here being so low, it was able to glide, like you just saw."

Franky did not understand what connection Emily was attempting to make between evolution and Collective Inception. "So what does all of this have to do with Collective Inception?" he asked.

"Okay, I just wanted to make sure you understood evolution. Like I was saying, in nature, everything normally tends to move toward disorder, chance and randomness. These creatures in the field, they live and die along with that same idea - everything that happens, good or bad, is a result of pure chance. One day a stampler happened to be born with a very useful weapon on its head. Wings. This change was very beneficial against its favorite prey, the rutliv. The problem was, that this small rodent-like animal, soon went extinct after the stampler learned to fly. The point is that it is survival of the fittest out in the forest. These animals don't ponder the right and wrong of the annihilation of an entire species. They just eat and live until one day they too are prey. But you see, nature respects that attitude. It's called evolution, survival of the fittest, right? When these animals play out their hunt, they are interacting with nature and fulfilling their duty as a member of the wild kingdom.

"This interaction with nature is most important. It is completely based on disorder, chance, and randomness. What was the chance that the stampler was going to develop wings? When it did, it wiped out an entire species. However, what also happened was a large drop in the number of stamplers. After the rutlivs were gone, many samplers simply starved. Today, the number of stamplers is less than it was when they didn't have wings! That's how nature keeps a balance through disorder. Random events cause good and bad things to happen. It's how nature attempts to perfect itself. Once a conscious intelligence reaches a Collective Inception though, nature recognizes itself in a perfect state and the need for change is obsolete. Evolution doesn't exist around a Collective Inception. And, no giant meteors, floods, or earthquakes, or any other random events will occur. Change through the process of evolution ceases.

"It's sort of like a cosmic evolution. Planets throughout the universe are bombarded with random catastrophes in an attempt to cause changes. This state of disorder is necessary to aid the evolution of species and continues until an intelligent species evolves and enters a Collective Inception."

"But you have square clouds, and perfect trees, how does nature become ordered?" Franky asked.

"What I just described, a Collective Inception, is a Social Order with a pefectly balanced polis. What you really want to know then is, how a well balanced polis causes nature to become ordered, as opposed to disordered. Right?"

Franky nodded.

"Everything you see, everything in the universe, is made up of small particles. The smallest of particles are called subatomic. These subatomic particles can change energy levels suddenly and randomly. On Earth, this is called a quantum jump. Basically, Franky, it is this 'quantum jump' that causes nature to tend toward disorder.

"Self aware creatures can interact with this quantum jump. When the polis is well ordered, the quantum jump lessens. A Collective Inception occurs only when the quantum jump no longer occurs in subatomic particles. That is why nature tends towards order when a polis is ordered." Emily said as she began to lead Franky back toward the house.

"The overall effect on a well ordered Social Order is amazing. Suddenly, the little things that citizens do to destroy nature's adversities become beneficial. Because my neighbor lived in my house while his was repaired, we became good friends, and he later helped me with my gardening. These little things combine to form a collective force in the society. Throughout the citizenry, the people grow closer together, all the while strengthening the Social Order, which in turn, further lessens quantum jumping, which in turns puts even more order in nature around that Social Order. This is why magnitude 7 through 9 Social Orders are referred to as spiral Social Orders. This collective force continues to grow until the social group becomes so spun together that nature is no longer disordered, and thus negative effects of nature are removed, and in fact, only positive effects of nature remain. It is at this point that a Collective Inception is reached for that society.

"However, for all this to even occur, or even just get started, a society must learn and practice Devout Reality. Pride, greed, and vengeance must be set aside so that the giving process can become the norm for each citizen. And as you know humanity just isn't ready for that yet. But, we are trying to, sort of, speed things up for humanity. Aliens are trying to do this in lots of different ways, and these lessons on Fathom Sound are just one of many. So now you know why it is so important that you do your best to help us, Franky."

Franky nodded, amazed at the size of the alien operation

on Earth. "Will a Collective Inception occur on Earth during the Earth Franky's life time?" he asked.

"No. However, I do know that soon, within his life time, a magnitude 7 will start! That will be a celebrated day among everyone."

By now, Franky and Emily had made their way back to the house. They ate lunch and continued to discuss Devout Reality through dinner and into the evening. That night, an exhausted Franky fell quickly asleep. His displaced memory had somehow put together the full extent of the alien operation, and as he slept his dreams made more sense to him.

Standing on the mountain side, Franky lowered his head into the brush, as the roar of the helicopters thundered above. He was drawn by the pyramid just below the ridge on which he stood. Quietly, he slid down to get a closer look. It appeared to be 200 feet tall, and maybe 200 feet wide. The lights here also seemed strange. Franky could not identify the light source. The light somehow did not cast any shadows off objects in the area. The light seemed to glow out of the air in a circle around the entire platform.

Franky cautiously stepped onto the platform's surface. Seeing no one, he approached the pyramid through the night air. As he did, he could see what looked like an enclave that had a doorway. Quickly, he walked over to the opening in the base of the silver structure. Above the doorway he saw the familiar polis symbol. As he stepped into the structure, a desert suddenly surrounded him. Off to one direction, he could see a cloud rising above the horizon. Stretching his vision in that direction somehow lifted his feet off the desert surface. He parted the surface quickly, and heard a growing sound of what seemed to be thunder. Looking off toward the cloud, his vision took him there.

Closing in on the smoke, Franky identified the cause. A wild herd of thousands of animals marched across the desert surface in perfect rows, twenty-three across. Like a machine, they stormed in perfect order, all in rhythm with one another. The thunderous sound of the thousands of feet smashing the ground at the same time put Franky into a trance.

Then, without warning, a long, pale, thin, arm of an alien reached from behind Franky and pulled him out of his trance, ending both ride and dream.

Franky sat up out of bed sweating. His heart racing, Franky now completely understood the meaning of his previous dreams. He had made some deep seated connections that no one expected or hoped he would. He realized that the pyramid structure was a learning device used by the aliens to simulate dream-like events that had Devout Reality meanings. Because of its location, shielded by the mountains, anyone inside it would remember those dreams, or visions, with an undisplaced memory. Sound can not travel through mountains easily, so the tainting sound waves would be stopped short of the pyramid. He figured that the shape of the pyramid had something to do with the high frequency sound, maybe to reflect any stray waves. It was obviously very important to the aliens that whatever the students saw in the structure, they remember. He also wondered if Egyptians and Mayans imitated the pyramid structure of their dreams by building the great pyramids on Earth. All of this made him more determined then ever to remember what he learned for the Earth Franky, as he asked in a previous dream.

More than ever, Franky became determined to enlighten humanity his way, even if humanity, as Emily pointed out, was not quite ready for such an enlightenment. Franky did not just want to change human nature, but to do it quickly. By exposing the physics of Devout Reality, he hoped people would see the wrong in pride, greed, and vengeance. "It all seems possible," he thought that night as he laid in bed. If only he could pass on these undisplaced memories to Franky.

Franky spent the last few days with Emily never revealing to her his detailed memories of Fathom Sound. And as the five days of lessons came to a close, Franky said his good-byes to Emily. He knew that after he fell asleep, he would wake-up the next day a different person.

However, Emily had a different parting in mind. "Let's go for a walk," she said as she walked toward the back door.

They stepped out into the backyard, and climbed the path that led into the darkening woods. Emily continued, "We are going to say good-bye in person." Confused by this, Franky soon understood as they came up over a hill. Down about 100 yards lay a familiar ship. The silver disk sat silently.

"Franky," Emily started, "it has been nice knowing the Earth you. I hope you were not too upset by all of this," she said as a tear filled up in her eyes.

Franky could do nothing but hug her. Together, they cried a tear and gave a laugh to break up the parting.

"This is silly," she said wiping away a tear. "It's only your mind that is going away."

Franky looked up at Emily, "You know, I will always remember you, despite all of your attempts!"

Emily shook her head and smiled. "And I will always remember you. So go on, and make that change you promised yourself," she said with a bigger smile.

Shocked, Franky could only crack the corners of his

mouth into a smile. "Thank you," he said as he turned and started his walk. Taking just a few steps, he stopped and turned around for one last look, only to see that Emily was already gone. When he turned back toward the ship, two alien beings were before him. Reaching out to them, Franky was no longer afraid. His disruption on Fathom Sound had forced their introduction, which in turn eased his fear.

As the ship skipped out of the planet's atmosphere, Franky wondered how this whole process was going to occur. They led him to a room where another alien stood. One alien looked off to one direction suddenly, the wall opened up, and Franky could see they had already reached their destination.

A bright light poured in the ship's entrance. Franky walked to the door and stopped to gaze outside. Standing there, something touched his soul. He immediately realized that this place was special. No tropical flowers, or exotic animals were anywhere to be seen. As Franky stepped out of the ship, he stepped on what seemed to be the very edge of the world.

Franky found himself just a few steps away from a great canyon. Five steps forward, and Franky would fall 17,000 feet straight down the flat face of a mammoth cliff. In fact, as far as Franky could see around this place, all of the canyon cliff walls had 90 degrees of straight down awe-inspiring exhilaration. And 17,000 feet down Franky saw surprisingly nothing. Despite his gut feeling that this was a place of tremendous significance, he could not help but question why he was here.

Then, as if on cue, one of the aliens approached Franky from behind and put its pale thin hand on his goose pimpled arm. "Franky," the alien said non verbally, "this is the entrance way into our home. Down in that valley," while pointing down into the great circular canyon.

Confused, Franky just shook his head from side to side as if to communicate a lack of comprehension. The alien stepped forward to the edge of the canyon and stopped. Turning around it continued, "A day is coming for Earth. When it is here, we will meet again. Now, watch me Franky. Have not only understanding in what you have been taught, but have faith. Watch me, then see what you have been taught. Follow me, and have faith in what you understand."

Franky's mouth opened wide as he suddenly realized what the alien was about to do. To Franky's astonishment with its back to the canyon, the alien took one large step backwards. And then another step back, and then another. Before Franky could say anything, the alien had walked off the cliff and somehow managed to suspend itself 17,000 feet in the air, and as the alien floated there, it slowly raised both long thin arms into the air.

"Behold the powers of nature! I fly with no wings. This is the order around the entrance to our civilization. Now come, Franky. Step toward me, and truly find Devout Reality!"

Franky stepped to the very edge and gazed down the face of the cliff. He stared down below, and something in his soul broke his fear. As fear gave way to faith, he looked up to the alien and stepped off the cliff.

A powerful rush of air flowed up and further pushed Franky off the edge. Somehow though, he was walking on air. The air rushing up from below was so powerful, Franky's hair stood straight up, and he had to struggle to keep his arms next to his body. "Was the air powerful enough to keep me afloat?" he wondered.

Before he could ask, the alien grabbed his hand and pulled him even further away from the cliff. As the distance between Franky and cliff grew, the air flowing up slowed. Franky very suddenly began to fall straight down toward the valley below.

At first panic struck him. But as his velocity increased something within calmed him. He continued down, but as he quickly approached the valley floor, he noticed a sudden decrease in downward velocity as his body neared the side of the cliff once again. So much did the downward velocity decrease that he came to a complete stop only 100 feet above the valley surface.

To Franky's immediate right he saw a stone platform that he quickly stepped on. The platform was shaped like a ramp that extended down to the desert floor. He began to walk down it toward the open expanse of valley ahead. As he did, he noticed how light he seemed. He could leap twice as far as before. "The gravity must be low here," he thought as he skipped down the ramp. Looking off as far as he could, Franky still saw nothing that resembled a civilization. "This is their home? A desert?" he thought.

However, it was not long before Franky realized that there was something out there. At first he wasn't sure what he was seeing. And then, before he could do anything, he walked into something hard. Shocked he reached his hands to touch the invisible wall. It shimmered after the initial impact Franky had with it. "Is it a mirror?" he wondered. That's the way it looked, except it did not reflect back his own image.

Franky ran his hands along the wall looking for a way around. Then suddenly, the air around him began to glow bright white. It continued till he found himself completely engulfed. At that moment, Franky lost his body, identity, and his state of being. He felt himself rise up out of the canyon, and off of this planet. Stars rushed away from him until they all spun together to form a single point of light. And when they did, they exploded into one bright light, which is where he found Devout Reality for the first time. The entire past, present, and future of the universe merged into one single realization. He saw all places within the universe, every beach on every planet, every sun of every solar system. He saw all of these places through out their history. He saw all of the universe in one single moment. Time and space lost their meaning. All places and all times in the universe were merged as one. Since space had no meaning to him, he could no longer understand distance. Thus, the unified universe could not be visualized as something any distance away from him. He had become part of the universe, he was one with all. This was the alien home, and the home of cosmic consciousness. Through this timeless spaceless state, the consciousness of all self aware creatures in the universe resided. Here, he could understand the power of the cosmic consciousness fully.

Then without warning, Franky was back in his body beyond the city walls. Standing on the valley floor, he was indeed enlightened beyond comprehension. What's more, he completely understood Devout Reality for the first time. Despite Emily's teaching abilities, Franky could only understand the theoretical aspects of Devout Reality before, but now, he understood the reality of Devout Reality. Like pieces to a great puzzle, the mysteries all fell into place to form a grand picture of that reality.

Franky turned around to see the ship was now on the valley floor near him, and he walked to it and entered. Looking around the room he spotted the alien who lured him to the cliff's edge. Franky nodded his head to thank it.

As the ship's door closed, the alien told Franky that now he was going to his home. Finally, they were going back to Earth. Deep inside, Franky wondered if he was going to be able to remember anything at all. In any event, it was not going to be long before that question would be answered. Franky could see that the ship had already arrived as the ship's wall melted away exposing a very familiar and Earthly night scene. He immediately recognized this surrounding. . .

Franky slept in his southern New Jersey bed. At ten years of age, he could not comprehend what lay ahead. A noise like a rhythmic pounding rang out from inside his head. He covered his ears with a pillow in a worthless effort to quiet what he knew was the beginning of another abduction. Resisting commands in his head were futile. Uncontrollably, he sat up in bed in a trance.

Outside, and 100 yards down a hill, lay a silver saucer shaped craft. A white light pierced the spaces in the curtain of his window as he slowly made his way through the dark house toward a basement door located in the kitchen. Light invaded from under the door and key hole. Reaching up, he turned the dead bolt lock, and opened the door.

Filled up with light, he could see the shadow of the creature cast on the opposite wall as it glided up the stairs toward him. With a numbing sensation on his spine, he froze, as he waited for the inevitable confrontation. A touch from the creature on Franky's head, and all else was forgotten.

Franky sat on a table in the ship swinging his legs calmly. They had just landed on Earth, one alien had departed but had not yet returned. "Where did the other one go?" Franky asked an alien next to him.

"To get your clone," it answered.

Franky stopped swinging his legs as the alien came into view approaching the craft. With the alien, walked a dazed Franky. The Franky in the ship slipped off the table with amazement.

There they stood, face to face. Not really sure what to think. Franky said, "Hello," to the dazed Franky, but got no response.

The aliens directed both Franky's to another room. Like in his dreams, this room had two tables with tall white walls that curved into a ceiling. At the top, tinted windows wrapped around the base of the ceiling. They laid down on separate tables that were positioned next to one another. The aliens then began to touch the backs of each of their heads. Soon afterwards, with a sudden jerk, a wire was placed into the back of their heads. The dazed Franky looked terrified, but paralyzed. He looked straight up toward the ceiling, and then slowly glanced down at the wire leading from his head. The dazed Franky followed the wire leading into the wall then out of the wall and up to the back of the other Franky's head. It was then that the dazed Franky began to stare at his twin in a puzzled look. To the dazed Franky's horror, the other Franky then said, "Hello."

With that the dazed Franky turned toward the ceiling. A sudden, slightly painful, flash of light pulsed in both of their vision. Their bodies jerked, then rested. Both were seized unconscious. One alien lifted the Earth Franky, and slowly carried him back to the house. The Earth Franky awoke as the alien entered the yard. Still in some sort of trance, he quietly entered the house. Back in bed, he shook off the trance, and fell quickly asleep, unaware of what had happened. . . but then, he awoke out of his sleep, as if some faint memory jarred his brain. And for the first time in his life, he opened his eyes. . .

Chapter Eight

Awakenings

"Many abductees engage in a lifelong search for answers to questions they cannot fully formulate. For some, the New Age movement (wherein spiritual and humanistic values are achieved through alternative pathways to conventional learning) provides an answer. In some way they know they are in contact with a 'higher' or 'cosmic' consciousness."

-Dr. David M. Jacobs
"Secret Life"

October 24, 1976.
6:40 a.m.

℡ he sound of distant call grew louder in his head. "Franky, get up!" the voice called from behind a door, "Come on, breakfast is getting cold!"

Franky rolled onto his feet as the morning sun lit up his room. He rubbed his eyes. Slowly, Franky made his way into the kitchen.

"I didn't think you were ever going to get up. Didn't you hear me? I've been trying to get you up for the last half hour," his mother asked.

"No," he said with a dry voice.

"And your father left the house like a hurricane this morning! I can't believe you. What's the matter with you, anyway? This is the third time this week you overslept."

"Must be those hot dates that he's been sneaking out for late at night," his older brother Casey said with a chuckle.

"Shut up, stupid!" Franky said to him sarcastically. "I had that bad dream again, mom. The one with the skeleton man down the basement," he said as he looked up at the basement door dead bolt. "That's why I'm tired."

"Again? Maybe you better not eat any snacks before bedtime anymore," she said as she placed a plate of french toast in front of the two brothers. "You better eat quick, your bus will be here soon. I've got your clothes downstairs in the dryer," she added.

Casey looked up at his mother. "Mom, you better let me go down and get them. That skeleton man has a nasty bite!" he said with very serious tone.

"You're such a goober!" Franky said getting up from the kitchen table. He walked angrily into his room and laid back down on his bed.

After a few minutes, his mother opened up the bedroom door with an arm full of clothing. "Here's your clothes," she said as she laid them on the bed next to him.

Then as Franky sat up, she noticed a dark spot on his pillow. "What's that?" she said as she picked up the pillow. A small nearly dry wet spot appeared to be blood. "What's this from?" she asked.

"I don't know," he responded.

"Turn around," she said as she visually scanned his head. As he did, she probed her fingers along the back side of his head.

"Ouch!" he yipped when she centered on a small pimple like bump on the lower part of the back center of his head.

"Looks like you got a pimple! Won't be long, and you'll be driving," she said as her concern shifted to humor.

Franky loaded into the school bus and departed for class. Franky was in the 5th grade, and as he pulled into the parking lot he could not help but notice the skeleton card board figures posted to the school entrance door. "Man, I hate that dream!" he thought as he pulled open the door.

Mr. Adams had a class of 25 students of which Franky was one. On the board was the day's agenda. The first was 'Show and Tell'. It was at that point that Franky realized that he had forgotten to bring in his rock collection. "Now what am I going to do?" he wondered. Then it occurred to him to tell the story of his repeated nightmares. It was nearly Halloween after all, and maybe the class would think the dreams to be as frightening to them as they were to him. So, that's just what he did.

"Franky. You're up!" Mr Adams announced.

Franky walked to the front of the class. "I forgot my show today, but I have a tell. Um, and it's about a dream I keep having. For like the past month, I've been having the same dream, almost every night, where this skeleton comes up from my basement and gets me. He lifts me up on my back and tickles me on my stomach down the basement!"

"What's it look like, Franky?" Mr Adams asked smiling.

"Sort of like the skeleton decoration at the schools entrance. Only scarier!" he said drawling a few laughs from the class.

Toward the end of the day, Mr. Adams elected Franky to wash the blackboard. Franky went out of the room to fill up a bucket of water, and when he return, he walked past his desk. There, sitting at his desk, was the cardboard cut of a human skeleton. Its arm was raised, as if it were waving at him. Inside, Franky thought that the incident was funny, but the class thought it was hilarious. So Franky played along. He acted shocked, and jumped back. This only caused the class to roar further with laughter. Even Mr. Adams rolled with laughter.

However, Franky realized something right there and then. It was not a skeleton man in his dreams. The creature he saw did not have exposed bones in the rib cage. Nor did it have a jaw with large teeth. In fact, the mouth was small, very small. A skeleton man description only seemed to be an easy way of naming a familiar image that visited with him regularly.

*   *   *

July 26, 1993.
1:00 p.m.

The church room was filled to capacity on the day Franky married Rebecca Ann Holiday.

This was no small wedding. The Holiday family was notoriously wealthy, and they loved to show it off. The wedding, afforded completely by Rebecca's parents, was just one more way to demonstrate it.

Rebecca's Father, Edger, was one in a long line of conservative wealthy Holidays. He owns Holiday Reality. Besides homes in West Palm Beach, and Cape May, they live in southern New Jersey. In a town named Haddonfield.

Rebecca's Mother, Rachael, was educated at Harvard, and practiced law with a local firm.

Rebecca Ann Holiday and Franky Carter met in their junior year, at Eastern High School. Just in time to choose colleges together. Both were accepted to the Florida Institute of Technology in Melbourne, Florida. Rebecca wanted to major in a biology field, possibly Marine Biology. However, Mr. Holiday, demanded that she be more "realistic", and "keep career minded". She graduated in 1988 as a chemical engineer. In the summer of 1988, Mr. Holiday found her a job with a pharmaceutical company in Trenton, New Jersey. She's the bread winner.

Franky started to fly airplanes at the age of fourteen. He was sixteen when he earned a private pilot's license. For some unexplained reason, flying is what he always wanted to do. Despite Mr. Holiday's recommendations to the otherwise, he elected to major in Aviation. When he graduated in 1988, he held a Commercial Pilot's license, Multi-Engine Rating, Instrument Rating, and Certified

Flight Instructor Certificate. In the spring of 1989, he landed a job as a flight instructor with a small flight school at Red Lion Airport, in southern New Jersey. Unlike his wife, his pay is minimal. In fact, he had told Rebecca that after the honeymoon he was going to look for a second job.

Franky's mother, June, was a housewife. At one point she drove a school bus, but for most of Franky's life, she was the typical housewife. His father, Thomas and brother Donny, were cabinet makers, working with a unionized firm called London Interior.

Franky's sister Elizabeth, everyone called her Liz, was the oldest of four Carter children. Liz, fresh out of medical school, never had time for relationships and was still unmarried.

Casey, a New York City cop, is Franky's other brother, and is married with two daughters. He is a New York City cop.

The Holiday family is very small, and Rebecca is an only child. In fact, the church at the wedding was filled almost completely with Franky's relatives. The reception immediately followed the wedding ceremony, and was held at the Holiday home. The weather was ideal, 84 degrees and sunny. Mr. Holiday would've had it no other way. Fully catered, complete with over two dozen servers, Mr. Holiday boasted that the event ran in excess of $45,000. A full orchestra was cast in the background. At the very center of the yard laid a large white tarp covering something that is not normally present in the yard. A long rope ran from the center of the tarp up to a tree branch, than back down to a small stage podium. A simple pull on the rope would reveal what kind of massive gift lay underneath the tarp. It was one of two wedding gifts to Franky and Rebecca by the Holiday parents.

After everyone had arrived to the reception, Mr. Holiday, in his usual dramatic style, took the podium, "I want to thank all of you for coming here today, on this beautiful day, to help Rachael, myself, Tommy, and June, wish the very best to two great kids, Rebecca and Franky. I know that this may be a little premature, but, I just can't wait to pull on this rope. This is a gift to Franky," he said as he began to pull on the rope causing the tarp to lift.

Under the tarp emerged a full sized, FAA certified, two passenger black glider, with silver lettering on the tail section that spelled, 'Black Bird'. To this everyone had some stunned reaction. Some clapped, while others simply gasped. Rebecca hugged a flabbergasted Franky.

"I would have gotten him an airplane with an engine, but you all know Franky, he may never have come back!" Mr. Holiday said with a laugh.

Midway through the event, Mr. Holiday called Franky into the house. There he asked him to have a seat in the den. Franky was expecting the old 'You better take care of my daughter' speech but instead received a business offer. "Franky, you know I consider you as my own son," he said as he poured a glass of scotch for himself. "Now, I'm not getting any younger, and I'd like to keep Holiday Reality in the family. I plan on retiring in a few years, and maybe living in West Palm full time. What I'd like you to consider is coming on board Holiday Reality. Learn the business, from the ground up. I'll pay you a good salary, and when I'm ready to retire, you and Rebecca can take over. I don't know if I need to tell you that last year Holiday Reality brought in nearly a seven digit income for Rachael and I," he said studying Franky's reaction.

Franky sat calmly. "That's quite an offer, Ed. I'll have to think about it for awhile. But I guess that would mean

I'd have to give up flying."

"Who says?" Mr. Holiday snapped as he poured another drink. "Now, I'm not saying that you'll have time to instruct, but hell, you could buy a fleet of planes with the money you'd make. How much you ever gonna make instructing? Ten dollars an hour? If your lucky, maybe. Look, I'm not gonna pressure you to do anything. Go on your trip, relax, have fun, and think about this offer. But remember one thing - this is a one time offer. I need to start training my replacement soon," he said with a sincere look.

Franky knew that there was money in the offer. It was an opportunity that most people would jump at. The trouble is, Franky had little interest in becoming wealthy.

The reception went smoothly. A five hour party, it was only broken up when Franky and Rebecca had to depart for the airport and their honeymoon. They were scheduled to depart Philadelphia International Airport on USAIR Flight 138 bound for Fort Lauderdale Florida at 9:50 p.m.

Franky was now 27 years old. He stood five foot, ten inches tall and had short straight brown hair with brown eyes. His wife, Rebecca, also thin, had straight brown hair and brown eyes. Rebecca was tall for a women, also standing at five feet ten inches. They hurried off the plane and onto the late night Fort Lauderdale Airport. They retrieved their rental car, and made their way toward the hotel along the beach.

As they found their way up along highway A1A, they located the Ocean View Hotel. It was smaller than they had envisioned, but they didn't care too much for detail by that late hour. Although Rebecca did briefly complain that they should have taken her fathers offer to stay at the Holiday's West Palm Beach home. After checking in, they rushed inside exhausted, and unpacked.

July 27, 1993.
2:30 a.m.

Franky felt odd the first night in the hotel. Maybe it was because it was a strange bed. There in that hotel room, 1200 miles from home, with the rhythmic waves washing on the beach in the background, Franky suddenly awoke. "What was that?" he said to himself as he lifted his head slightly off the mattress. As he lifted his head off the pillow to gaze toward where he thought he heard the noise, he saw some movement in the dark shadows. The noise and the motion seemed to be near the bathroom entrance. Franky wondered if it was his tired vision, or maybe just a large rat.

The hotel's security lights located outside the room provided some light in the room. Though the curtain was closed, there was a split up the middle creating a light streak across the room and onto the opposite wall, which happened to be to the immediate left of the bathroom entrance. Suddenly, Franky saw another movement as something large crossed the streak of light near the bathroom entrance. "That's not my imagination!" he thought. "And that's no rat, either!"

Franky froze, afraid to make a noise, or a motion that might let whatever was in the room know that he was awake. He could feel his heart begin to pound as the weight of his head began to strain his slightly lifted head.

Quickly, Franky thought of options. He thought to simply reach over and turn the light on, but decided that he might fumble too much with the light since it was completely shrouded in darkness. He thought to tap his wife until she awoke, but then decided that she might wake too loudly. Finally, he figured it would be best if he simply acted as if he were asleep. He figured the movement was due to a prowler that somehow gained access to his room. If the prowler came too close to him or his wife, he'd use the element of surprise and jump the prowler.

Then suddenly, another movement appeared out of the bathroom. "Two prowlers?" Franky fearfully concluded. But then horror gripped him as the one movement settled in the direct path of the light streak, exposing its identity. Frozen in fear, Franky was staring not at an animal, or a prowler. In fact, what he was looking at was not even human! With his heart in his throat, he wished that he could lay his head back down and close his eyes. He could not, if he made any movement now, they would see that he was awake.

They stood about five feet tall. Like mirrors, their large dark eyes reflected all the rooms available light. Something about the creatures seemed familiar to Franky. They were indeed the same creatures of his childhood nightmares, yet at that moment he could not recall those long ago dreams.

Then without warning, one turned toward Franky, as if somehow it suddenly realized that he was watching. It cast its eyes at him and froze. The two of them, shocked to see each other involved in a staring match, increased his tension and fear. Then the other creature turned toward Franky, as if it too somehow realized that he was awake. "Sleep," Franky heard softly.

"Are they whispering to me?" he wondered.

"Sleep," he heard faintly again. But Franky was not about to do that! His adrenaline was flowing beyond its limits, there was no sleeping now.

"Don't move," he then heard them somehow whisper from across the room.

Franky at this point became increasingly fearful. "Why

don't they want me to move?" he wondered.

"Don't move," he heard again. But before he could decide what to do, they both rushed him in unison. Instinctively, Franky jerked up out of bed and screamed, "THEY'RE COMING!" One reached out to grab him, and in that single moment, they disappeared. Rebecca awoke to his scream with her own heart now racing to the alarming yell.

"What! What is it?" she said frantically.

"They were . . .they were just here," he said reaching for the light.

"Who? Who was just here?" Rebecca asked.

"There were these. . . these things," Franky said as he began to inspect the room with the light on.

"What are you talking about? What are you looking for?" Rebecca asked as her sudden fear turned into annoyance.

"I heard a noise and saw these, like, people over by the bathroom. And then they, like, tried to attack me," he said confused.

"People? You saw people in here?"

"Well, sort of. Except they were mutants or something. They had huge dark eyes. They were skinny little things."

"You had a dream, honey. Come on back to bed," she said as she rolled back on her side.

"I guess so. I guess that's what it was. Pretty strange, huh?" he said as he slowly got back in bed.

"Yup. Goodnight," she said as she closed her eyes.

And as Franky turned out the light, it struck him where he had seen those creatures before. They were the skeleton men he saw as a child in his childhood nightmares. "The skeleton man!" he mumbled.

"What?" Rebecca asked agitated.

Franky looked over and saw the light streak that was still cast across the room. He then quickly reached over and turned the light back on. "What kind of dream configures the dreamers actual setting exactly the way it is?" he asked.

"Go back to sleep!" she said as she covered her head with a pillow.

"I've seen those things before. When I was little, I use to have these dreams all the time, where the same creatures would take me down the basement and like tickle me. It was the same creatures," he said as he sat up.

"Great. Now turn off the light," she said from under the pillow.

Franky turned off the light, but couldn't sleep. Rebecca on the other hand fell quickly asleep. The creature images stirred up the distant memories of his skeleton man visitations, although he still believed them to be weird dreams. After all, how could the skeleton man be real? The whole event was eerie to him. Franky waited for the sun to rise pondering this question, and trying to remember more details of his childhood nightmares.

"They like to sneak up on me," he whispered to himself on more than one occasion. "When my eyes are closed, that's when they come. There's no stopping 'em then."

Franky realized that this was paranoia talking. He also realized that he needed sleep. But underlying that early morning muttering, he sensed that somehow there was a degree of reality to the dreams, and to his rambling.

Rebecca was surprised to find Franky awake, showered, and clothed. "Want some coffee?" he asked.

"Thank you," she said nodding. "What are you doing up so early?" she asked.

"I couldn't get back to sleep after that dream," he said as he poured her coffee.

"Dream?   What dream?" she said reaching for her coffee.

Franky paused. "What do you mean, what dream?" he asked with squinting eyes.

"What? Did you have a nightmare or something?"

"Yeah! You don't remember it?"

"No. Should I?" she said sipping her coffee.

"Well, you had a conversation about the dream with me last night. And you were mad as hell about me screaming and leaping out of bed. So, I say, yeah! You should remember it!"

"Well, whatever, I don't! You want to go out for breakfast?" she asked trying to change the subject.

After breakfast they took a walk on the beach. Even though they were newlyweds, this was not the first time for a vacation together. So some of the excitement was taken out of the trip. Still, it's always nice to get away. That is exactly how they treated the trip. They both promised to do something different - something to set apart a honeymoon from a vacation.

When they walked up on a parasail stand on the beach, they glanced at each other and knew that this was it.

Rebecca went up first. As she landed, a smile on her face indicated to Franky that a good time was just ahead. This was different then flying. Attached to a parachute, he was exposed to the open air. It was different enough to get an adrenaline rush. After the first few moments in the air, Franky began to look around the Fort Lauderdale beach area. The morning sun glared off the ocean, and reflected back to him off some of the shore line hotels.

Then, he spotted a sparkling building far off beyond the beach. The image reminded him of something from his childhood. He did not realize it at the time, but a doorway in his memory was opened the night before. The recall apex of Fathom Sound was beginning to reveal itself. Though he could not explain why, the word, 'Memphis' came to his mind.

Chapter Nine

Forget Me Not

"The fact remains, however, that for thirty years, and possibly longer, thousands of individuals who appear to be sincere and of sound mind and who are seeking no personal benefit from their stories have been providing to those who are willing to listen consistent reports of precisely such (alien abduction) events. Population surveys suggest that hundreds of thousands and possibly more than a million persons in the United States alone may be abductees or 'experiencers,' as they are sometimes called. The abduction phenomenon is, therefore, of great clinical importance if for no other reason than the fact that abductees are often deeply traumatized by their experiences. At the same time the subject is of obvious scientific interest, however much it may challenge our notions of reality and truth."

-John E. Mack, M.D.
Harvard Medical School

July 28, 1993.
9:30 p.m.

Franky flipped through the cable channels on the hotel television, hoping to find something interesting, when a startling image appeared on the screen. "That's it!" he yelled. "Rebecca, come here! Hurry!" he hollered.

Rebecca rushed into the room, "What?"

"That's them! That's what those creatures looked like from my dream last night. . . and from my nightmares when I was little!" he said pointing at the television screen. On the screen was a film entitled, "Communion", a film based on an account of an alien abduction.

"Yuck!" she said as she turned back toward the bathroom, "They're creepy!"

Mesmerized, he slowly sat down in front of the television screen. He hardly blinked throughout the film. Any interruptions Rebecca made as she passed between the bedroom, bathroom and kitchen were not heard by Franky. After the film, he re-stated to Rebecca that the creatures on the television screen were the same as when he was a child.

"So what are you saying? They were aliens from another planet? That your dreams were real?" she said with raised eyebrows.

"Hey, I'm the last person in the world to believe stupid stuff like ufos, but still, how do you explain it?" he asked.

Rebecca paused, "Maybe you saw a movie like this and

you had a nightmare."

"Come on! Don't you think I'd remember a movie that horrified me so bad that I had the same nightmare over and over again? Which brings up another point, why would I have the same nightmare over and over again?"

"Maybe you were terrified by that movie," she said as she shrugged her shoulders.

"Or terrified by something else," he said seriously.

Rebecca's mouth dropped open, "You're not serious? You can't really believe what you're suggesting!"

"I don't know. We're talking, like, twenty years ago. Who knows what it was? All I do know is that those dreams happened over and over again when I was little, and a couple of nights ago, those things came back, only this time it happened in this hotel room," he said defensively.

"They're just dreams," she said as she changed the channel.

"What you don't understand is how seeing those creatures on T.V. makes me feel uneasy. I hate to admit this, but that movie scared the crap out of me!" Franky said thinking that was significant considering horror movies did not phase him in the past. Rebecca also knew this fact.

Rebecca tried to change the subject, but Franky could do nothing but think or discuss his apparent nightmares and the movie. They went to bed early that night, partially because Rebecca grew tired of Franky's obsession. Rebecca rapidly fell asleep, while Franky spent several hours tossing and turning. Much was on his mind. Every time he closed his eyes, fear forced them back open. Each time he opened his eyes, he half expected to find an alien leaning overtop of his head, staring down on him. Of course, when he opened his eyes, he was happy to find only a dark room. Finally though, he fell asleep.

Franky opened his eyes. He was standing in a desert. "Where am I?" he wondered. He turned around, scanning the horizon, looking for some sign of civilization. "What happened to the hotel?" he mumbled to himself.

A few feet up ahead, he spotted a small muddy pool of water. He walked over to it and glanced into the water. "Water? In a desert? Must of rained recently," he thought.

Then he noticed his reflection in the water. He was a child! As his mouth dropped open in disbelief, the water began to become rippled, causing his image to blur. Slowly, a low pitched sound began to grow, as did the ripples on the surface of the water. Franky looked off in the direction to which it seemed the sound was coming. In the distance, he could see a plume of what appeared to be smoke rising on the horizon. The sound continued to grow until it was a thunderous rumble.

Franky realized that he must be dreaming. The weird thing was that it seemed very real. He could feel the sweltering heat on his back and the wind was blowing tiny grains of sand into his face. The other notable thing about this dream was that it seemed familiar to him. As he looked around, he could not help but feel as if he had been there before.

Suddenly, he lifted off the ground as the sound became very loud. From his new height, he could see what was causing both the sound and what appeared to be smoke. A stampede of a strange looking cattle marched across the desert. This caused dust to be thrown into the air giving the earlier appearance of smoke. What amazed Franky was the number of the strange cattle, and the way they stormed across the desert. In perfect rows, twenty-three across, they marched in harmonious order to one another. A veteran army division of soldiers could not march any more in step with one another.

Just as quick as he was in the desert, Franky now found himself, laying on a table in a white room. The room was so quiet, he could hear his own heartbeat. The white walls rose up 30 or 40 feet then tilted inward slightly, then leveled off to form a ceiling. Just below the ceiling, black tinted windows encircled the room.

Franky felt a pain in the back of his head. He reached back, and felt a wire actually plugged into his head. Slowly he turned his head toward the left. He knew what he'd find. It was all quickly coming back to him. Laying next to him, was Franky as a ten year old boy, also with a wire connecting to his head.

"I remember this dream," Franky said aloud as he turned back to face the ceiling. Through the tinted windows, he could see images of the aliens of his nightmares. "But is this a dream?" he wondered. Fear raced through his body as his heart pounded harder. Then out of the corner of his eye, he spotted movement to his right. As he turned to see what it was, he was horrified to find an alien rapidly approaching him. "Nooooooo! Leave me alone!" he yelled.

"Leave me alone!" he screamed as Rebecca snapped him out of his dream. Franky sat up in bed sweating profusely.

"Are you all right?" she asked.

Franky turned the light on and glanced down at the clock. It was 2:30 a.m. With the light on, Rebecca could see that Franky was trembling.

"Um, I don't know. Bad dream I guess," he said shaking.

"What was it about?" she asked.

"Those stupid aliens, again! I don't know what's wrong with me!" he said rolling out of bed. "I can't sleep, that's one thing for sure," he said as he walked out of the room.

Franky put on a pot of coffee. Rebecca followed him into the kitchen. "What exactly was the dream about?"

"I don't know. Something about a desert and mutant cattle, and an alien operating room or something. I really don't know. It really doesn't make sense. I think I must be going nuts or something."

"Well, I wouldn't say that, but maybe there is something to all this," she said as she sat on a bar stool.

"You mean you believe in the alien thing?" he asked stopping what he was doing.

"Of course not. But maybe there's like something wrong in your childhood that's just now coming out for some reason. I don't know either, but Uncle Walt might be able to help," she said.

Rebecca's Uncle Walt was a psychiatrist. Normally, this suggestion would have offended Franky; however, he and Walt were close. Besides, Franky was truly worried and shaken by the last week's events. In two days they'd be home. Franky told Rebecca that he'd think about her suggestion.

August 2, 1993.
1:30 p.m.

The hot afternoon sun beamed relentlessly down on Franky and his student as they preflighted their aircraft. It was a small two passenger Cessna 152. Franky told his student, Keith, to complete the preflight as he walked over to talk to a close friend, and fellow instructor at the airport, Robert Onelliouski. Nearly everyone called him, Bob-O.

"What's up, Bob-O?" Franky asked.

"Not much. I saw your glider. Must be nice!" Bob-O said with a grin.

"Look who's talking, you got a real plane, with two engines!"

"Yeah, well, it's in the shop for right now. Is that thing of yours made of fabric?" Bob-O asked.

"Yup. It's an all fabric body. Lighter that way."

"Taken her up yet?"

"Nope. When you get your monster out of the shop, you'll have to give me a lift," Franky said.

Gliders of course need another plane to tow them to a specific altitude. Once a designated altitude is reached, the glider is released. Depending on weather conditions, and geographic conditions, a glider can glide ten miles of horizontal space for every 1000 feet of altitude.

Bob-O was a good friend of Franky's. They had been instructors at the airport for the past four years. Bob-O moved out of Texas to attend a local college, where he did his flight training, and got a job right after graduating. Bob-O would fly his twin engine Beech Duchess to Texas to visit his family during holidays and vacations. His parents were wealthy, owning several auto dealerships, and two sports bars.

Keith finished the pre-flight and Franky jumped in the planes right seat. They started the engine, put their headsets on, and taxied to the runway. Keith lined the plane up on the center line of the single runway and applied full throttle. Soon, they were airborne. Shortly after departing the airport area, Franky had Keith navigate to another airport. The sky was mostly sunny, but for a few isolated clouds.

About a half hour into the flight, as he scanned the area, Franky noticed a strange looking cloud about 1000 feet below, and behind the plane. It appeared to be perfectly square, as it disappeared from view underneath the planes tail.

"Cut the throttle to 2200 RPM, and do a right one eighty, to one-six-zero degrees," Franky abruptly snapped.

"What?" Keith asked confused.

Franky quickly took the controls and began the one hundred and eighty degree turn, "Thought I saw something."

"Like what?" Keith asked.

"It was a cloud."

Keith looked at his instructor even more confused. "There's more up ahead, why'd we have to turn around?"

Franky was entranced and didn't answer Keith's question as he frantically scanned the area now in front of the plane. "It was right here!" Franky said disappointed not to find the square cloud.

"What was right here?" asked Keith.

"It was a square cloud."

"Oh. That's weird," Keith replied.

Franky never found the square cloud, but seeing it gave him that familiar feeling that he was looking at something that he remembered seeing as a child. More and more, Franky was coming to realize that something did happen to him as a child. And with every screaming nightmare, so did Rebecca.

Rebecca knocked on the front door. After a few moments, a forty something, slightly overweight, man opened the door. "Rebecca! How was your trip?" he asked as he stepped out to hug her.

"Well, that's kind of why I'm here, Uncle Walt," she said hugging him.

"Come on in," he invited.

The house was centered in an upscale neighborhood of Haddonfield. The house would easily go for $650,000. A two story Victorian mansion seemed to be perfect for a therapist who did much of his work out of his home. Walt married into the Holiday family, but even though his wife died several years before, he was very much a part of the Holiday family functions and gatherings.

After getting some soft drinks from the kitchen, they sat in the parlor. Rebecca cut right to the heart of the matter and told Walt about Franky's nightmares.

"I think he should come and talk to me, or another therapist, but he should definitely talk to someone about this," he said seriously.

"If he even found out that I told you about the nightmares he'd kill me. Isn't there anything I can do?" she asked.

"If he's having nightmares with the frequency and at the intensity that you describe, no. He needs professional help. I think you should just sit him down, and get him to see me about his dreams."

"There's one other thing. I think he is actually starting to believe that the aliens in his dreams are real! Like they attacked him or something when he was little," she said uncomfortably.

"It's difficult for you?"

"Well, yeah! I'm always tired because come 2:30 he's screaming or leaping out of bed. Sometimes he can't sleep, so he stays awake half the night. It's getting to me!" she said.

"No, I mean about him believing that his dreams are real?"

"Kind of. I mean, it's not like I can say to anyone that my husband believes that little green men are after him. They'd think he's insane, so shouldn't I if he really does believe it?"

"I don't like to use the word insane. He may be confused

about some event or events that happened when he was a child. Or maybe he witnessed something horrible and his memory has suppressed it. Or maybe it's nothing at all, and he's just having some stress related dreams. Remember, he did just get married!" he said with a smile.

Rebecca smiled, "You're probably right."

"Well, I'm glad you feel better. Now, how about that hubby of yours, can you get him in here?"

"I'll try. That's the best I can do," she said as she stood up. "Thank you."

"The pleasures mine," he said as he poured her some coffee. "Sit. Have some coffee."

Franky and Rebecca were renting an apartment, even before they were married. They lived about ten miles from Haddonfield in a two bedroom split level apartment. When Rebecca got home, she was surprised to see that Franky had finished work so early. Upstairs, he was typing a letter on their computer.

"Done work so early?" she asked.

"Yeah," he said not volunteering that he canceled the rest of his lessons for the day.

"What are you doing?" she asked.

"Just finished typing a letter," Franky replied.

Sitting on the computer desk, Rebecca noticed a new book. She turned it over to reveal the cover, 'Hidden Lives, Documented Cases of UFO Abductions' by Ronald P. Jarodson, PH.D. "What's this?" she asked.

"That's where I'm sending this letter. To this Dr. Jarodson guy. Apparently, there are special therapists who deal with alien abduction cases. So I'm sending this letter requesting a list of nearby therapists who can help me."

"What? What happened to Uncle Walt?" she said raising her voice.

"Oh come on! I'm not about to tell anyone in your family that I've been abducted by aliens, I've decided that I just can't do that!" he said as he proof read the letter.

"So just how did you come to this extraterrestrial conclusion?" she asked becoming upset.

"I just can't explain it to you, you just don't understand," he said as he addressed and stamped an envelope.

"No! I understand. I understand that my husband thinks he's being visited by little green men at night and he doesn't think it's strange!" she said as she picked up the envelope off the desk.

Franky grabbed the envelope out of Rebecca's hand and walked to the steps, "And I have a wife who wouldn't know she had a dog if it bit her! And they're not green. They're grey," he said as he began down the stairs and out the front door.

The phone rang just has Franky pulled away in his car. Rebecca answered.

"Hey Rebecca, it's Bob-O. How ya been?"

"Well, I've been better," she said looking out the window.

"What's wrong?"

"Oh nothing, just an argument with the old man," she answered.

"Listen, I don't mean to change the subject but, I have one of Franky's students on the other line, he wanted to know if he could reschedule for tomorrow. Is the old man around?"

"You just missed him. He canceled his flights today, didn't he?" she asked.

"Uh - I don't know," he said slowly.

"You don't have to cover for him, Bob-O. I know the score," she said as she slammed the phone down.

September 22, 1993.
5:00 p.m.

Over the last two months, Franky's nightmares
continued off and on. Much to Rebecca's displeasure, he
told Mr. Holiday that he would need a little more time to
consider his business proposal. Meanwhile, Dr. Jarodson
had responded to Franky's request and Franky had
scheduled an appointment with a therapist in Philadelphia.
Only a twenty minute drive. He arrived shortly after 5 pm.
Franky had to calm the tensions between he and Rebecca by
not talking about his dreams. He also decided to keep the
visit to the Philadelphia therapist a secret.

Franky half expected to find a fortune teller type office
with a receptionist who handed out 'next in line' tickets.
Instead, he found a large private office on the eighth floor
of a center city Philadelphia high rise. "Dr. Randolf Skye,"
he read on a Harvard Degree hanging on the wall.

"You must be Frank Carter," a voice said from behind.

Franky turned around to find a thin clean shaven man in
his thirties approaching him with his hand extended.
Franky shook his hand, "And you are Dr. Skye?" he asked.

Dr. Skye nodded, "Call me Randy. Follow me," he said
leading into the back office area.

Franky sat down in a comfortable leather chair. Dr.
Skye picked up a tablet and sat across from him. Dr. Skye
quickly wrote a few brief notes on the tablet then set it
down. He then picked up a small tape recorder and pressed
a button, "I tape record everything we say. The tape will
always stay in this office. Is that okay?"

"Yeah, I guess. As long as no one else hears the crazy
stuff that's gonna go on it!" he said with a nervous chuckle.

"No, no, it'll only be heard by you or me. That's it! So

why have you come to see me?"

Franky readjusted his position in the chair and began explaining both his childhood and adult nightmares to Dr Skye. He then explained how upset he was when he saw the movie, "Communion" and told him about the square cloud incident. After Dr. Skye was certain Franky told him about every detail he could remember, he asked him how his wife was taking the whole thing.

After a lengthy discussion about Rebecca and her family, the focus moved on to his job. Dr. Skye wanted to know everything from how he got the job to how well the business was doing. It became clear that Dr. Skye was trying to determine if there was any change in Franky's life that could have caused these memories to surface. The stress of a wedding was a good possibility. Then Dr. Skye moved on to Franky's childhood nightmares. He asked about Franky's family history, and about how close he was to various members of his family.

An hour had passed, and Dr Skye hadn't found a cause to Franky's nightmares. Still, this was only one session. In some cases, it may take weeks, months or even years to uncover the cause of severe physiological trauma. Dr. Skye did view this as moderately severe, and thought hypnosis might be helpful in this case.

Franky was surprised that Dr. Skye avoided discussing aliens. After all, it was Dr. Jarodson's book about alien abductions that brought him to this office. Certainly, Dr. Skye knew that Franky was wondering about the possibility that he was abducted as a child, so why was he avoiding the issue? Finally, at the conclusion of the session, Dr. Skye mentioned alien abductions.

"Franky, you have to understand that these sessions may take weeks or months to solve the mysteries to your nightmares. I know that you have contacted Dr. Jarodson, and he has sent you to me, but you have to realize that the cause of your dreams is very much unknown at this point. Alien abduction cases are complex, and some of the patients who come here, thinking that they were abducted as a child, find that they were in fact not abducted. Then again, others find that they may have been. But you have to be willing and able to handle the results of your search for the truth. First we will figure out what has caused these nightmares, and then most importantly, we will figure out how to deal with the cause. That is the part that is sometimes the most difficult. Can you handle whatever we find out about your past?" he asked seriously.

"Yes. I have to know."

They scheduled another appointment for the following week.   Dr. Skye asked Franky to wear comfortable clothing, like sweatpants and a light shirt. He also asked Franky to avoid anything stressful the day before and the day of the next visit. They were going to attempt hypnosis.

September 29, 1993.
5:20 p.m.

Franky laid comfortably on the cloth sofa. Dr. Skye had managed to get Franky to relax, which is the key to successful hypnotic regression. Hypnotic regression is used to access a patients unconscious memories of the past. In some cases, it can be successfully used to recover distant memories several decades old. After a few minutes of relaxing meditation, Franky was ready.

"Okay Franky, now I want you to go back to when you were young. Go back to the night you had a nightmare. You are ten years old now, and you're having a dream about a skeleton man. Can you see it?"

"Yeah," Franky answered softly.

"What does it look like?"

"I'm still in my room."

"Is the skeleton man there?"

"No."

"What are you doing?"

"I'm holding a pillow over my head."

"I see. Why?"

"The noise is coming," Franky said as his heart rate increased.

"What noise?"

"It's like - banging. Like someone's coming up the steps. Bang, bang, bang," he said rhythmically.

"Okay. Can anyone else hear it? Like maybe mom and dad?"

"No. They're sneaky like that."

"No? How do you know?" Dr. Skye asked.

"They're only after me. OH GOD! THEY'RE COMING!" he said raising his voice. "I told you. The banging means they're here! Please make them go away," he said as his lips began to tremble.

"It's okay. Everything's okay!" Dr. Skye said as he made sure that the tape recorder was still recording.

"What's happening now?"

"I'm walking toward the kitchen," Franky said with a shaky voice.

"How did you get there?"

"I walked there."

"Is anyone with you?"

"No. I'm alone," Franky replied.

"Where are you going?"

"To open the door to the basement."

"Why?"

"I'm not sure why. I guess they want me to."

"Who are they?"

"The skeleton men. Now there's light coming up from under the door."

"Light? From the other side of the door?"

"Yeah."

"What do you do now?"

"I'm opening the door. I don't want to . . .please don't hurt me! Please!" Franky said as a tear rolled down his face.

"WHAT'S HAPPENING!" snapped Dr. Skye.

"Ouch! No, I know, and I don't care. Please, not tonight! I don't want to!" Franky said quivering.

"Franky! Tell me what you see! What do you see?"

"It's the skeleton man! I told you he was coming!"

"What's he doing to you?"

"I don't know. He's doing something to my back and stomach. Ouch! And to the back of my head! Now it tingles."

"What does the skeleton man look like?"

"I'm afraid to look at him! I try not look at his face."

"It's all right. You're safe. Everything is okay. Now, when I count to three, I want you to take a peak at his face. I want you to tell me what he looks like. Okay?"

"I've got my eyes closed. I don't want to!"

"It'll be okay. You'll be safe. I'll count to three, okay?" repeated Dr. Skye.

"Okay," Franky finally said after a pause.

Dr Skye began to count, "One, two, three. Now take a peak!"

"Oh no! I told you. It's the skeleton man. He's ugly. Please no!"

"It's okay! Good! Now what did he look like?"

"He's white. Bright, um, maybe greyish. But very bright. Big dark eyes. He's just staring at me. I don't like when they stare at me. He gets inside my head."

"What about his nose and mouth?"

"Little. . . little tiny nose, like a dark hole in his face or something. And his mouth is like a crack. Real small. . . No! I don't want to!"

"What? What don't you want to do? Is he talking to you?"

"Yeah."

"What's he saying?"

"He's saying,'everything is okay', and he wants me to come with him outside."

"I see. So you are not outside yet?"

"No. We're down the basement."

"Oh. Okay, what happens next, then?"

"We're going outside."

"Did you tell the skeleton man that was okay?"

"No. I told him that I didn't want to go outside."

"So he's making you go?"

"Yeah."

"How?"

"He tells me that it's safe, and then my legs just start moving. I can't stop them from moving!" Franky said calmer.

"I see. So you're outside now?"

"Yeah. We're going to his space ship. But I'm looking at my legs and I can't stop them from moving."

"Okay. How far away is it?"

"Just down the hill, behind some trees."

"Can you see it?"

"A little bit. Like I know about where it is, so I just look over there, and I can kind of see a little bit of light there."

"Is the skeleton man next to you still?"

"Yeah."

"Is he touching you, or just walking next to you?"

"Um. He's like a little behind me, I think. Yeah, he's like right next to me, but a little behind me too."

"There is only one skeleton man with you?"

"Yeah."

"Where are you now?"

"We're almost at the ship."

"What's the ship look like?" Dr. Skye asked as he picked up his note book and pen.

"It's like shiny."

"Metal?"

"I guess. But it looks funny. Like silver liquid or something."

"How big is it?"

"It's pretty big. Like as wide as the house."

"Oh. What's it shaped like?"

"It's round. The edges are sharp. At the top, there's a bump. It raises higher than the rest of the ship. The metal looks like water, it's really shiny, like a mirror."

"You said there was a light, where is the light coming from?"

"Under the ship. There's a low purple light."

"Okay. What's happening now?"

"We're next to the ship and like part of the wall disappears, and now there's a ramp leading into the ship."

"Do you go into the ship?"

"Yes."

"What does it look like inside?"

"It's all white. There's two other skeleton men waiting for me."

"What do they want?"

"I don't know."

"What's going on?"

"They're taking me to another room . . ." Franky said then paused.

"What's the new room look like?   Is there any furniture?"

Franky didn't respond.

"Franky! What do you see?" snapped Dr. Skye.

"I missed you," said Franky as a flood of tears poured down his face.

"Franky! Who are you talking to?"

Franky smiled. "I didn't think I'd ever see you again," he continued.

"FRANKY!" Dr. Skye yelled, "Who are you talking to?"

"Emily," he replied.

"Whose Emily?"

"My other mother," he answered as he wiped the tears from his face.

"Your other mother? What does she look like?"

"She's got blond hair - it's in a pony tail. She's real pretty."

"What are you doing?"

"We're hugging."

"How do you know that she is your other mother? Where have you met her before?"

"On Fathom Sound. And at home."

"Fathom Sound? Where is that?"

"I don't really know. It's like thousands of light years away or something."

"You've been there?"

"Mm-hmm."

"You said you met Emily at home before. Does she

know your parents?"

"No! Not that home. My home in Atlantis."

"Atlantis?"

"Mm-hmm."

"Where is Atlantis?"

"Not too far from Fathom Sound, I think."

"So you got two homes? How can that be?"

"Ah, my twin clone really lives in Atlantis, we just kind of share the memories of it. So I feel like I've been there."

"Clone?"

"Yeah. The alien Franky lives in Atlantis, but shares his memories with me. I guess it's the ultimate exchange program," Franky said with a smile.

"Okay Franky, I want to bring you back now," Dr. Skye said quickly. "You're now older, its 1993, and you're in Dr. Randolf Skye's office. When I count to three I want you to open your eyes, okay?"

"Yeah."

"One, two, three, now open your eyes."

Franky opened his squinting eyes. Quietly he sat up on the sofa. "Franky, do you remember what we just talked about?"

"Yes," he said emotionally numb.

"How do you feel about all of that?"

"I remember everything now. After I tell you what I'm about to tell you, you are either going to commit me to a hospital, or laugh."

"I can assure you that none of that will happen."

Franky's complete memory of Fathom Sound and Atlantis had returned intact. Details of all the lessons learned were also remembered, including his journey around the mountain. Franky began to describe the incredible journey and adventure, much to the amazement of Dr. Skye.

They spent the remainder of the evening discussing Fathom Sound, Devout Reality, the polis, Atlantis, Troy Bolger and Emily.

"Franky, I know a few people who could confirm some of the physics that you learned on Fathom Sound. You said something about gravity, and how it curves space-time. Do you remember how?"

"Yes. In every quark, a sub-atomic particle, exist a quantity of negative volume. This naturally displaces the positive volume around it, causing the curvature. The more quarks, the more displaced space-time around them. That is how gravity curves space-time, which of course is how it forces planets into orbits around large bodies like the sun. Gravity is a result of space-time being curved, as Einstein proved in 1905. But how is it curved? Negative volume. This means that the heavier an object, the more negative volume it has, and the more space-time it displaces. Surrounding positive volume would be pulled closer, in all directions, toward negative volume. That is why mass warps space-time."

"Okay. I think I understand. I will pass this anonymous theory on to see if it holds water," Dr Skye said as he finished writing down some notes.

Dr. Skye then began to probe Franky's emotional side. He wondered how he was taking all this. He also knew that it would take many months and even years to resolve any emotional distress that these apparent abductions have caused. Dr. Skye also asked Franky to bring his wife on the next visit which was scheduled in two weeks.

Dr. Skye then handed Franky a piece of paper with a name on it - Daisy Sanchez. "This is the head of a support group for abductees like yourself. I think that it would be a good idea for you to call Daisy up, and meet with the group. I think they meet the last Tuesday of every month."

Franky agreed. He was emotionally drained, but happy that he finally knew what had been happening to him as a child. He also wondered if the aliens had returned to him as an adult in the hotel room in Florida. Or, was that a real dream? And could he find Troy Bolger? These were questions that he figured he would get answered the next meeting.

Chapter Ten

Treason

"The governments of the major nations have assembled countless dossiers about the (U.F.O.) subject. In the course of military and intelligence data gathering, many remarkable facts have been accumulated, as we know from the few tidbits the U.S. government has been forced to release under the Freedom of Information Act. Yet officials have never seen fit to declassify most of the files."

-Jacques Vallee
"Revelations"

October 14, 1993.
8:00 p.m.

𝕿he interesting thing Franky learned on his most recent
visit with Dr. Skye, was that there actually was a
Troy Bolger who lived in California. Dr. Skye was also
able to learn that this same Troy Bolger once lived in
Sacramento, and that his father was and still is in the Air
Force. Franky also learned that his theory involving gravity
was plausible, and while unprovable using today's
technology, attracted a great deal of attention from the
Harvard Physics staff. So much so that one professor
asked if a meeting could be arranged.

Days before the most recent session with Dr. Skye,
Franky had told Rebecca about the therapist, and asked if
she would go with him to the next session. Rebecca became
very angry, and referred to Dr. Skye as a 'quack.' Rebecca
shared this development with her Uncle Walt, and she then
asked that he confront Franky when he returns from Dr.
Skye's office. With some hesitation, Walt agreed.

Franky pushed open the front door to his apartment.
Sitting in the living room was Walt and Rebecca. "Hi
Walter," Franky said surprised to see him.

"How you been, Franky?" he asked.

"Good, and you?" Franky returned.

"Never felt better," he said as he caught a stare from
Rebecca.

Franky also saw the look Rebecca gave Walt, "What's going on here?" Franky asked.

"Franky, Rebecca tells me you been seeing a therapist," he said uncomfortably.

Franky returned his own stare at Rebecca, "Yeah, and Rebecca's got a big mouth, too!"

"Look Franky, this may be none of my business . . ."

"You're right, it is none of your business!" Franky snapped.

"Franky!" Rebecca yelled, "I asked Uncle Walt here! I'm worried about you! You're becoming obsessed with this alien crap!"

"You see! That's the problem here! You want to label me insane. Well, I'm sorry to disappoint you both, but I'm not crazy," Franky said as he put his notebook down on the table.

"Nobody's labeling you. Nobody's saying you're crazy. Rebecca's is just upset by all this. I think a calm discussion would help matters greatly," Walt said as he motioned Franky to take a seat. "I'm not here as a psychiatrist, I'm here as a friend."

"I'm sorry Walt, but it's comments like, 'alien crap' that hurts," Franky said as he sat down across from Rebecca.

"I'm sorry," Rebecca said softly as she tried to fight off the tears that were filling up in her eyes.

"Okay. Now that's a start. Now, why don't you tell me about some of the therapy you have been receiving. Whose the doctor?" Walt asked.

"Dr. Randolf Skye."

"Randy Skye? I know him. We've attended seminars together. He seems like a good fellow. Harvard graduate, right?"

"Yeah, that's right," Franky said as he looked at

Rebecca, "Harvard," he repeated hoping to get Rebecca's attention.

"I heard," Rebecca announced, "that doesn't mean he can't be a quack."

"That's enough!" Walt said. "We need to be able to communicate without slighting one another. Now, how has the therapy gone thus far?"

"Good. I'm now sure that I was abducted by extraterrestrial beings as a child. Next week, I'm going to a support group where other abductees meet, WITH THEIR UNDERSTANDING SPOUSES, to discuss their trauma," Franky said again looking over at Rebecca.

Rebecca looked away.

"Rebecca. I know that this is all very hard for you, but for the sake of your marriage, I think that you should consider going with Franky to this support group. It may actually help you, if you meet other spouses. I'm sure that they are having the same problems with all this that you are having."

"Wait a minute!" she yelled as tears fell from her eyes, "How is it that I have a problem? I asked you to come here and talk to Franky, not me! He's the one with a problem."

"Go to hell!" Franky yelled.

"Hey!" Walt snapped at Franky. He then turned toward Rebecca."Rebecca, you're wrong. You both have a problem, and unless you are both willing to deal with it, it's not going to go away."

"I'll go," she said softly as she wiped the tears from her face.

Franky's shock stunned him.

"Good, there's hope," Walt said, "When is it Franky?"

"October 30th, it's a Tuesday."

"I want you to clear your schedule for that night, okay

Rebecca?" Walt asked.

"Okay," Rebecca said softly.

October 30, 1993.
7:00 p.m.

Rebecca and Franky knocked on the front door of the two story home. Ironically, hanging on the door was a card board cut out of a human skeleton. The door opened, "Hello. You must be Mr. and Mrs. Carter?" the woman assumed as she opened the door and welcomed them in. She was an attractive Hispanic women with long dark hair in her early thirties. "My name is Daisy Sanchez, come in and have a seat."

Franky and Rebecca walked down the steps and into the lower level where they found a large room with 30 or so chairs. Already, 20 or so people had arrived and were in active conversation with one another. This was not what Rebecca had expected at all. She had envisioned a handful of rejects. Instead, a room full of adults, some obvious professionals still wearing suits apparently coming to the meeting directly from work. It was also obvious that Franky and Rebecca were new to the group because everyone seemed to know everyone else.

As they stepped toward two empty chairs, a woman and man approached them. "Hello. This is my wife Judy, and my name is Howard. This is your first meeting, right?"

"Yes," Franky said nervously, "My name is Franky and this is my wife Rebecca."

Rebecca gestured a hello.

"Come on, let me introduce you to everyone," Howard said as he waved Franky and Rebecca closer to the rest of the group. "Everyone, this is Franky and Rebecca, this is their first meeting."

The group gave their warm greetings. Then one by one, Howard introduced each person to Franky and Rebecca. They were amazed at the levels of professions sitting in the room. Three doctors, including a surgeon, two police officers, two construction workers, a receptionist, a lawyer, seven administrators for various company's, four management professionals for various businesses in the local area, a dentist, and a computer programmer. Add flight instructor, and chemical engineer to that list.

The home owner, Daisy, returned from upstairs with a tray of snacks. A large coffee maker was located in one of the room's corners on a table. Daisy had overheard much of the introductions.

"Now that you know everyone, I want to lay a simple ground rule down, that everyone here has agreed to. Whatever you hear here tonight stays here. It's that simple. You don't mention names to friends, or discuss what was said, outside of this house. This is for both your own protection as well as ours," Daisy said as she passed the tray of snacks around.

"Protection?" Franky asked.

"Yes. As you can see some of us here could be professionally injured if some of this stuff ever got out. You're a flight instructor, right?" Howard asked.

"Yeah."

"Well, I'm sure your students wouldn't like to hear that their instructor is seeing little green men. Am I right?"

"Yes, okay. I understand. You don't need to worry about us saying anything to anyone," Franky announced.

"Good."

Daisy sat down and began the meeting, "Now, where did we leave off last meeting?" she asked as she turned several pages in her notebook.

Howard jumped in, "Why don't we hear what brought Franky and Rebecca to our meeting first?"

"Oh yes! I'm sorry, where's my head tonight? Would either of you like to share with us your situation?" Daisy asked.

Franky nervously stood up. "It's me. I've been seeing Dr. Skye the last few months, and he and I have discovered that I was abducted as a child. It's been very hard to deal with . . . for both my wife and I. We've been fighting, and attacking each other. I'm afraid to believe half the stuff I'm finding out through hypnosis, and Rebecca refuses to believe any of it," he said shaking.

Most of the group nodded their heads slowly as if they all could relate to their situation. Daisy slowly looked over both of Franky's and Rebecca's faces. She read the honest pain in their eyes. "8 out of 10 abductees report that their initial abductions occurred as a child. Your story is very familiar to us all. And Rebecca, ask anyone of the spouses here, they have all been through what you're going through."

Despite Rebecca's efforts to keep the tears back, they rolled quickly down the sides of her face. "It just all sounds crazy, you know?"

"I know. But some of the latest surveys conducted by a broad band of psychiatrist and researchers, have estimated that several million Americans may be abductees, like your husband. So it's not weird or unusual, it's just not socially or politically acceptable. But whether or not it is acceptable doesn't change the fact that it is happening or happened to millions of Americans," Daisy responded.

"What do they want?" Rebecca asked.

"That's the million dollar question. We can only guess.

Some of the women abductees report that their ovaries are fertilized, then later a fetus is removed by Greys, then brought to full term in a tube."

"Greys?" Rebecca asked.

"Aliens! Extraterrestrials," Howard interjected.

"They're called Greys because of their off white appearance," Daisy continued. "Whatever their intentions, they have the capability to do it. Their technology far exceeds anything man can even dream of."

"Why doesn't the government do something. I mean they must know, right?" Rebecca asked.

"They know!" Howard answered. "How could they not know? Just look at Roswell."

"Roswell?" Rebecca asked.

"Yeah, way back in 1947, Roswell New Mexico," a man said from the back of the group.

"In 1947 a UFO crashed in the Desert, just outside of Roswell," Howard started, "The wreckage was recovered by the military. The next day, the Army base's commander reported to the local paper that they had recovered a crashed UFO! Of course, once a General got news of this, the story changed that it was really a downed weather balloon."

Daisy interrupted, "Till the day he died, the officer who was first on the accident scene, Major Marcel, said that the weather balloon story was crap, and that there was a cover-up."

"Witnesses to the event were threatened bodily harm by the military to themselves and their families, so the cover-up was successful up until the late 1970's when finally many of the witnesses spoke up. Of course many of the witnesses were by then in their 60's, 70's or even 80's. But still, there are nearly a hundred living witnesses to the Roswell event that say that it was a recovered UFO," Howard said.

"But why the cover-up?" asked Rebecca.

"They're afraid the public will panic," someone from the back said.

"I think they're afraid of them," Howard said with a chuckle.

"More likely they don't want to admit to the public that they can't protect us from them," Daisy said.

"The government made a deal with them," Franky said softly. Everyone turned toward him.

"I've heard that one before too. How do you know?" asked Daisy.

"My story's kind of long, but I'll try to keep it simple. Basically, when I was about ten years old, I was abducted. The next thing I knew I was on some island called Fathom Sound. There, these humans were teaching each child something called Devout Reality. It has a lot to do with social dynamics and how consciousness can affect nature and physics. So for five days I learned all I could about this Devout Reality. But then one of the instructors explained how the students' memories were affected so that when they were back on Earth, they would not remember Fathom Sound consciously. They use some sort of high frequency sound wave that you can not audibly hear. They create this sound continuously so that any memories made while subconsciously listening to this sound can be located in the brain, and displaced - sort of forgotten on a conscious level. When I heard this, I snuck out of the camp and around a mountain, where the sound waves couldn't travel. So unlike most other abductees, my memory of Fathom Sound has not been displaced."

Most of the group sat with open mouths. Franky realized that even other abductees may find his story hard to believe. "What do all childhood abductees have in common?" Franky asked. "Dr. Skye told me that they all believe that they are in touch with a cosmic consciousness. They also tend to believe in social harmony. This is the basis for Devout Reality. They don't call it Devout Reality, but they understand it. The government did recover a UFO in 1947. And the aliens offered a deal with the US Government. Keep the abductions quiet, and we will supply you with some technology every 10 years."

"Oh come on, Franky! Why would the Grays, who are far more technologically advanced, need to get permission from the US military to make abductions? They could do whatever they want, whether we allowed them or not!" Howard argued.

"True. But, you missed the point. They were not asking for permission to do anything. They were buying the military's mouth. The aliens wanted the abduction process to remain hidden from the public, not because they want permission but because if Devout Reality is ever to work on Earth, it has to start with people wanting to do it. And as you know, it is very much human nature to resist anything that is forced, regardless if it is good intentioned."

"This story is still hard to buy," Daisy admitted.

"You know what? I don't care if you buy it or not. It's the truth," Franky said defiantly.

"You said something about physics. Do you remember any of that?" someone from the group asked.

"I remember everything. I could tell you how gravity works, why quantum jumps occur randomly within atoms, the shape of the universe, and how to travel faster than the speed of light," Franky replied.

"Have you given any of this physics knowledge to professors yet?" asked Daisy.

"Yes. Dr. Skye asked me to right it all down, and he

gave it to a professor at Harvard University. So far, the professor is impressed, and he is sending the theories to some other professors at other institutions," Franky said.

"Well, if what you're saying is true, and if I were you, I'd be careful," Howard said.

"Careful?" Rebecca asked.

"He means if the government ever found out that my head contained information that could prove that there is a cover-up, they'd probably spare no expense in shutting me up," Franky said.

"And if these theories are being circulated, how long do you think it's going to take before someone asks where all these blockbuster theories came from?" Howard asked.

"Who is the government anyway? I mean whose in control, the President?" Rebecca asked.

"Well, when we talk in terms of UFO cover-ups, we are talking about the military," Howard answered.

"Yeah, but, the military answers to the President, right?" she asked.

"There are factions within the military that answer to the intelligence branches of the military. The center for this rogue military is said to be at Nellis Air Force Test Range, at Groom Lake, Nevada. It's nicknamed Dreamland," Howard said.

"Dreamland!" Franky exclaimed. "That's the name of the treaty the government made with the aliens, 'The Dreamland Alliance'. Every ten years since December 23, 1963, the military has been meeting the aliens to receive computer technologies."

"I'd bet that's where the meeting is happening, at Groom Lake. It's one of the most secure military locations in the world, centered in the Nevada desert, north of Las Vegas. There is no way of getting in, and even if you did, you'd never get out - alive. I saw a documentary on this base once, there are signs around the perimeter of the base that say, 'Trespassers will be treated with deadly force'. In the center of the test range, exist a base called, Area 51. It has the longest runway on Earth. This is the place some call Dreamland. The latest technologies are tested there, and until very recently, the military denied that Area 51 even existed."

"So, are you saying that the President doesn't know that aliens are abducting people?" Rebecca asked.

"I don't know. The thing I can say for certainty is that people are being abducted, and the public and the government refuses to take it seriously," Howard answered.

After the meeting, Franky and Rebecca drove home. Rebecca pleaded with Franky to tell her father about the abductions, but Franky refused. He figured that if the theories were proven accurate, then he could go public with his abductions, but not before. Rebecca agreed to keep the whole situation to herself. At least she was sympathetic to Franky's story now. She still held some reservations about the matter, but for the first time considered the possibility that aliens had indeed abducted her husband as a child.

November 23, 1993.
5:00 p.m.

The black limousine did not stand out in the business high rise section of Philadelphia. Parked, the driver remained at the wheel. In the back seat sat an adult male in his early thirties. The dark suit he was wearing demonstrated both his taste in style and his wealth.

Someone knocked on the back window from the outside. "Hey Mike, let me in," the man said.

"When is his next appointment?" Mike asked as the window slid down.

"5:15."

"All right Pete, get in the other side," Mike said as the window closed.

Pete stepped into the car, and placed a head set on his head. "What's the next ones name?" Mike asked while staring at the entrance to a high rise across the street.

"Uh, Carter. Frank Garrett Carter. Looks like he lives in Jersey," Pete said looking at an opened notebook. "I sure hope this is the one, I'm about tired of listening to all these wackos. I don't know how these doc's can stand it. I think I'd go crazy myself!"

Mike glanced down at his watch. 5:10. Without looking away from the building entrance, he reached into his jacket and pulled out a 9mm hand gun, released its clip of ammunition, glanced down to insure that the clip was fully loaded, then returned the clip into the butt of the gun. He then placed the weapon back into a holster, strapped to him, under his jacket. "Shut up, and just listen," Mike said coldly.

Pete frowned at Mike, who was not looking at him, then pressed the headset onto his head tighter. He then turned the volume control slightly. "I don't hear anything yet, just sounds like the Doc's up there," Pete said quietly.

Franky and Rebecca parked in a nearby parking garage and hurried down the block toward the high rise. They did not notice the black limousine parked across the street as they entered the building. They took the elevator to the eighth floor, walked down the hallway, and entered Dr. Skye's office.

"He's a really nice guy, you'll like him," Franky said whispering to Rebecca as they took a seat.

"We've got our 5:15!" Pete yelled.

Mike quickly reached down and put on his own headset, then slightly adjusted a volume knob on the side of the right earphone. "Okay now, don't say a thing. If they drop a pin, I want to hear it," Mike said quickly.

Dr. Skye heard Franky and Rebecca enter and came into the waiting room. "Dr. Skye, I want you to meet my . . ." Franky started then stopped mid sentence.

Dr. Skye immediately waved his hands wildly in the air in an attempt to quiet Franky. He then placed his finger along side of his nose. A prewritten note was then held up stating, 'IT IS IMPORTANT THAT YOU LEAVE NOW, I WILL EXPLAIN LATER'.

Franky and Rebecca looked at each other stunned. "What?" Franky asked.

Dr. Skye again lifted his hand up into the air, trying to quiet Franky. He then turned the note over, pulled out a pencil, and began to quickly write another message.

"What is that?" Pete moaned. "Sounds like . . . scratching or something."

Mike immediately put his open hand up in Pete's face to quiet him. A slight twist of Mike's head told Pete that he too heard the scratching noise. "That's not scratching," Mike said as his face turned tense and angry. "That writing! That bastard's writing notes!" he yelled as he threw down his headset and pushed open the back door. Pete followed him as he weaved through traffic to get to the high rise entrance across the street.

Franky and Rebecca could hardly believe their eyes as they read Dr. Skye's note, 'THIS PLACE IS BUGGED, LEAVE NOW!' Dr. Skye had tried to contact Franky earlier using a pay phone, but only got the answering machine. He left a message cancelling the appointment hoping that Franky would get the message. Unfortunately, they both came straight from work.

Immediately, Franky and Rebecca walked out of the office, as Dr. Skye followed. They walked toward the elevator and stopped.

"Keep going. You better take the fire exit. That'll lead you out the back of the building. There are some people watching for you at the entrance of the building," Dr. Skye said as he whispered and brushed the sweat from his forehead.

They opened the fire exit door. "Thank you!" Franky said. With a nod from Dr. Skye, Franky turned around and began to hurry down the steps with Rebecca.

Dr. Skye returned to his office, and closed the door. He hadn't gotten across the room when the elevator bell chirped. Halfway across the room, this stopped Dr. Skye in his tracks. He knew that someone had arrived on the eighth floor, and at 5:20, it was a rare event.

His heart raced as he heard heavy foot steps race to his door, and as the door flew open, Dr. Skye spun around to face the individuals.

"Where is he?" Mike yelled as he and Pete stepped into the office.

"Who?" asked Dr. Skye.

"Do I look like I'm playing games? WHERE IS HE!!!" Mike screamed as he whipped out his 9 mm and pointed it at Dr. Skye's head.

Dr. Skye trembled, "I don't know."

"Clear the hallway!" Mike said to Pete. With that Pete stepped into the hallway.

"You have to play hero don't you? Well hero, I'm going to give you 5 seconds to tell me where he is . . ."

Just then Pete burst into the office, "Mike! The fire exit

doors ajar! They must have gone down it!"

Mike scowled as his anger welled up from within, "Five!"

Dr. Skye closed his eyes as the two bullets entered his forehead. Lifelessly, his body hit the floor.

Franky and Rebecca raced to the parking garage and quickly jumped into their car. Rebecca emotionally distraught, burst into tears. "What's going on?" she cried.

"I don't know, but I kind of didn't want to stick around and find out," Franky replied.

As they drove out of the parking garage, Rebecca let out a yell.

"What?" Franky asked.

"Look at the building entrance!" she said as she slid down the seat in fear.

Franky turned and saw two men dress in dark suits run across the street and get into a limousine. Franky noticed a handgun in one of their hands. "I guess they found out. I hope Dr. Skye's all right."

"Dr. Skye? Dr. Skye? What about us? We've got some government people or something, chasing us, and you're worried about Dr. Skye?" Rebecca asked as she sunk down to the bottom of the seat.

"I don't understand. Why not just come to our house?" he mumbled. Then it hit Franky, "They didn't know which of Dr. Skye's patients I was! And now they know."

"Which means they know where we live!" cried Rebecca.

That point Franky realized also. His pulse jumped as he weaved through traffic to get onto the Ben Franklin Bridge leading back to New Jersey. After crossing the bridge, Franky's panic gave way to reality. Where could he run to? He thought about simply going to a police station, but was afraid of the uncertainty of what these people wanted. Did they want him dead?

"How about Daddy's? He knows some politicians! Let's go there," cried Rebecca.

"No. I don't think that even he can help us now! I've got a plan," Franky said as he stepped a little harder on the accelerator.

"Oh great! That makes me feel a lot better!" Rebecca said as she tried to compose herself.

"Listen, we're going to go home. As soon as we pull up, I want you to run inside and start gathering essentials. Make sure you have our check book, and all our credit cards. Actually, I guess we better stop at the bank and withdraw most of the money from our savings. Okay, gather what you can, throw it in our gym bag. I'll gather some clothes for both us. Then, we're going to the airport!"

"What? Airport?" Rebecca said as she sat up in the seat.

"Red Lion. I'll take the Cessna 182RG, and we'll get out of town for awhile," Franky said still thinking out the details.

"Why not just drive? At least we'll have a car when we get to where we're going," Rebecca asked.

"As we speak, I bet our tag is coming up stolen or something. Remember, these guys are probably part of the government! That's why I want to get to the bank, they might even freeze our credit cards and bank accounts. So when we get to the bank, you go to the ATM and get cash advances from our Visa and Mastercards, and I'll go get our savings account money. Okay? You with me?" Franky asked.

"Yeah."

They pulled into the banks busy parking lot.

Fortunately the drive through was open till 8:00pm. Franky let Rebecca out so that she could get to the ATM, while he pulled up to the drive thru window. There were two cars ahead of him, and the wait seemed to last forever. Finally, they had acquired what they could, $1900.00. Unfortunately, there was a $1000 cash limitation at the drive thru window. Rebecca had managed to get $300 from each credit card, she also pulled $300 from the checking account using their ATM card.

They raced home and pulled into the apartment complex parking lot. They both leaped out of the car, leaving the engine running. Franky gathered some clothing, a bag of fruit, and his flight bag. Rebecca placed what she could into the gym bag and that quickly they were back in the car.

With wheels screaming, they pulled out of the entrance of the main road that lead away from the apartment complex. Just as they stopped and waited for traffic to allow them out, their nightmare limousine appeared down the road coming in their direction.

"Oh my God, Franky! Is that them?" Rebecca screamed while pointing.

"I don't know," he said as he pulled out going the opposite direction the limousine was approaching. They passed each other, and it was clear that it was the same car. Franky looked into his rear view mirror. It was also clear that they saw Franky's car.

The limo's breaks screamed, as the black vehicle spun into a u-turn. "Hang on, and get down!" Franky yelled as he stepped on the gas pedal.

Franky obviously knew the area very well. He used this to a great advantage as he made his way in the general direction of Red Lion Airport. However, the limo continued to slowly gain ground on Franky and Rebecca, and as they neared to within a few miles of the airport, he knew that he'd have to lose the limo. When they approached a familiar intersection, Franky saw his opportunity. He knew that the limo could not take a turn as quick as his car could, so he hit the 90 degree intersection turn as fast as he could without losing complete control. He then made another quick turn down a winding rural road that ultimately lead to the airport. It worked.

The limo couldn't make the turn, and had to come to a stop and back up to the intersection road, and then turn. By that point Franky's car was no where to be seen. Mike and Pete continued to drive down one of the two possible roads that Franky and Rebecca could have taken.

Franky pulled into the airport parking lot and slammed on the breaks. "Get all this stuff into the blue and white one right there!" Franky said to Rebecca pointing at a plane. He then jumped out of the car, and ran into the airport building. Bob-O was turning out the lights to the office area of the building, when Franky burst into the building.

Bob-O turned around stunned. "You scared the crap out of me!"

"I need the keys to 45 Gulf," Franky said out of breath.

"What? What are you talking about? What's wrong?" Bob-O asked.

"Look buddy, I don't have time to explain right now, just give me the keys and I'll call you, Okay?"

"All right. No problem, but do you need any help?"

"No, just give me the keys!" Franky said as he lifted the horizontal blinds to take a peak outside.

"Here ya are. Have a good flight!" Bob-O said.

Franky grabbed the keys and as he stepped out the door, he stopped and turned back around, "Are you alone here?"

"Yeah, I was just about to leave. Why?" Bob-O asked.

"Get in your car and go home. Be gone before I take off. And if anyone ask, you didn't see me! Okay?" Franky asked quickly.

"What's going on Franky?" Bob-O asked with a worried look on his face.

"I'll call you! Now, just do as I say, okay?"

"Okay! Okay!"

Franky ran to the plane. Rebecca was seated and ready. "Everything loaded in the plane?" Franky asked Rebecca.

"Yeah."

As Franky started the plane, he turned around to see Bob-O drive off away from the airport. "What did tell him?" Rebecca asked as the plane slowly began to roll out.

"Nothing. I didn't tell him anything."

The single engine plane's lights twinkled in the evening, and as the plane neared the runway, Franky gave one more look back at the road in time to see the limo scream to a halt in front of the airport.

"The car! They saw the car!" Franky yelled as he hit the throttle causing the planes engine to roar to life.

The plane quickly rolled onto the runway just as the limo spun around and accelerated in the direction of the plane. As the plane pulled away down the runway, Franky looked behind to see the limo smash through a wire gate and roll onto the runway. As the limo neared them, the plane reached take-off speed, and lifted off the ground.

Moments later, a few soft pings could be heard. Fortunately, the 9 mm rounds did not find either Rebecca, Franky or a vulnerable spot of the aircraft.

Chapter Eleven

Black Within Black

"When, in the course of human events, it becomes necessary for one people to dissolve the political bands which have connected them with another, and to assume among the powers of the earth the separate and equal station to which the laws of nature and of nature's God entitle them, a decent respect to the opinions of mankind requires that they should declare the causes which impel them to the separation. We hold these truths to be self evident; that all men are created equal; that they are endowed by their creator with certain unalienable rights; that among these are life, liberty, and the pursuit of happiness; that to secure these rights, governments are instituted among men, deriving their just powers from the consent of the government; that whenever any form of government becomes destructive to these ends, it is the right of the people to alter or to abolish it, and to institute new government, laying its foundation on such principles, and organizing its powers in such form, as to them shall seem most likely to effect their safety and happiness."

-Thomas Jefferson
1ˢᵗ Part of the 'Declaration of Independence.'

November 23, 1993.
9:20 p.m.

Rebecca, attempting to sleep, rolled uncomfortably to her side. The planes engines had faded into a monotone hum by now. Franky quietly folded the aeronautical chart in front of him, taking care not to wake her. They had been in the air for two and a half hours and by now were just southwest of Pittsburgh. Franky used his flashlight to find a small airport on the map that had both night runway lighting, and refueling availability. He spotted the perfect airport in Washington, Pennsylvania. Fuel was no problem and there was a restaurant and motel nearby.

Franky woke Rebecca and prepared for the landing. "I had hoped it was all a nightmare," she said exhausted.

"It is," Franky responded as he hit a switch that lowered the landing gear.

They landed and parked the plane. It was too late to refuel because the small airport was closed. They called a cab using a pay phone next to the airport office, and within 20 minutes they were at 'Angelo's' restaurant filling their empty stomachs.

By 11:00 p.m. they were checked in at the local 'Best Western' and soon after, fast asleep. The trip had been exhausting, both mentally and physically. Still, both tossed and turned into the early hours of the next day.

November 24, 1993.
3:15 a.m.

Franky opened his eyes and stiffened his legs. Quietly, he sat up out of bed. He stepped to the door and walked outside without shoes on his feet. He made his way around the back of the motel where a patch of dark trees stood. Within the thickest part of the trees, a soft light glowed.

Franky climbed his way up an incline as he continued on toward the light. His barefoot slipped on the moist dirt, and down he went, forcing him to bump his head as he rolled back down the incline.

Franky laid still momentarily, then shook his head as he sat up. He looked around, wondering where he was. Then his hair stood up on the back of his neck when he heard a rustling noise in the trees at the top of the hill. Franky looked up and saw some branches swaying in front of a light radiating from within the woods.

Without wasting another second, he stood up and ran toward a parking lot light, which lit up the front of the motel. It was then that Franky realized where he was. Fortunately, he remembered his room number.

Rebecca woke up startled when Franky slammed the motel door closed. He frantically began to lock the door.

"What is now?" Rebecca yelled.

"They're out there!"

"The police?" she asked.

"No, the aliens," he said still trying to catch his breath.

Then a bright light lit up the outside facing curtains.

Franky looked over to Rebecca as he braced himself against the door. "Get ready," he yelled.

Rebecca ducked down behind the bed just as the light

disappeared. Then the bang of a car door slamming was heard. Rebecca stood up and walked over to the window and glanced out.

"It was a car. Just a lousy car."

"But, I saw a light in the woods," he said.

"Franky, look," she said pointing to a man and woman walking away from the car. "They're just people. Not aliens from Beta Rayticula, just humans like you and I."

She then collapsed back onto the bed. "Now go back to sleep."

Of course, Franky couldn't sleep.

November 24, 1993.
6:50 a.m.

"Franky! Where are we?" Rebecca asked as she tried to wake him.

"What?" he asked dazed.

"Where are we?" she repeated.

Suddenly, the prior days events flashed into his memory, as he jump up in the motel's bed. "South of Pittsburgh," he said. "Come on, we better get going."

"To where? Where are we going? Aren't we far enough already? They won't find us here, right?" she asked as she watched him jump in the shower.

"Sutter Creek!" he yelled from the shower.

"What? Sutter Creek?" she asked confused.

"Sutter Creek, California. That's where we're going," he said sticking his head out of the shower.

"California? Why? What's in California?" she asked as she walked into the bathroom.

"Troy Bolger," he replied. "We're going to go look for Troy!"

"Who?" she asked.

"He was a friend of mine on Fathom Sound. He won't remember me, but maybe he's aware that he's an abductee and we'll be able to remind him of Fathom Sound. His dad might be able to help us, he's pretty high up in the Air Force."

After breakfast, they went directly to the airport, refueled the plane, and paid for 'tie down' fees. Franky walked over to the pay phone and placed a call.

"Red Lion Airport, Bob-O speaking."

"Bob-O! It's Franky! Sorry about the fence, pal."

"Franky? Where are you? Man, you're in some deep shit! What happened?" Bob-O asked whispering on the phone.

"It's a long story, one that I'll tell ya as soon as I figure my way out of this mess. I'm gonna need the plane for a while, okay?" he asked.

"Franky, you know I can get locked up just for talking to you? Jesus man, did you shoot someone?" Bob-O asked.

"Shoot someone?" Franky said loudly. "What makes you think I shot someone. Some guys were shooting at ME!"

"Well, that's not what's all over the news! They're saying that you shot some psychiatrist in Philly last night," Bob-O said still whispering.

Franky could hear commotion in the background. "Oh my God! No! Is he all right?"

"All right? With two holes in his head? No he's not alright! He's dead!"

All Franky could do is drop the phone, and walk away in shock. These guys were cold blooded professional killers, and the worst thing about it was that they worked for the government. Rebecca watched from the plane as a pale, white Franky approached her.

"What's wrong?" she asked.

"Nothing. Put your seat belt on," he said in a monotone voice.

Faster than ever before, he had the single engine Cessna airborne. "They killed him! They killed Dr. Skye!" Franky said as the plane continued to climb.

Rebecca cupped her hands to her mouth, trying to hold back a gasping scream. Again tears rolled down her face. "Why? Why?"

"They want me," he answered. "Maybe I should just turn myself in."

"For what? You didn't do anything."

"They think I shot Dr. Skye!"

"What! With what? You don't even own a gun."

"You don't think that they placed the murder weapon in our apartment by now?" he asked.

"Well, we'll just tell them. We'll get a lawyer. We'll take a lie detector test!" she yelled as she wiped the tears from her face.

"Polygraph test are not admissible in a court of law," he answered.

"It's a good thing we got out of there when we did," she sighed.

They continued the flight west into Ohio, shocked and stunned, and officially on the run for a crime they did not commit. Franky calculated that he would have to stop six times so that they could refuel along the way to California. He hoped that no one was looking for him this far west, and that most of the small airports were not looking for his plane. He couldn't help feel that seeking out Troy for help was a long shot, but they were out of options, time, money and patience.

November 26, 1993.
4:00 p.m.

The cab pulled up to the affluent house. Franky got out
and asked Rebecca to stay in the cab. The Porche and
Lexus parked in the U shaped driveway gave Franky a
feeling that someone was at home. As he approached the
front door, it opened, and stepping out was a tall man in his
50's carrying a brief case. He was dressed in full military
dress blues, obviously an Air Force uniform. That's when
he noticed Franky approaching.

"Can I help you, son?" the man said with a deep voice.

"I'm looking for Troy Bolger. He does live here, doesn't
he?" Franky asked.

"Who are you?" he asked.

"Uh, my name is Frank. I'm an old school buddy of
his."

"Well, you won't find him around here. He left about
two years ago. He lives up on Mono Lake," he said as he
walked over to his Lexus and opened the door to put in his
brief case.

"Mono Lake?"

"Just off Rt 167," he said as he walked over to the
driver's side of the car. "That is if he's still there. I haven't
heard from him for over a year. Okay?"

"Yeah, thank you sir," Franky said as the man started
the car. Franky returned to the cab and ask to be taken to
a bus station.

"Bus? Why are we taking a bus?" Rebecca moaned.

"Troy doesn't live here anymore. Lives somewhere on
Mono Lake."

"Mono Lake? I know where that is!" the cab driver interrupted. "Ain't many people up there this time of the year!"

"Do any buses go that way?" Franky asked.

"Don't know for sure, but I imagine so. Long as the first snow hasn't hit, you may be in luck.

"Was that his dad?" Rebecca asked.

"Yeah, I think so. He really didn't say. But this is his parents address, and that guy seemed to fit the bill," Franky answered slowly.

"Did he seem nice?" she asked

"It seemed to me that he and Troy don't get along. He seemed not to care to much either."

After arriving at a bus station, they learned that a bus did depart for Yosemite National Park at 6:30 a.m. the following morning. Yosemite National Park was about 15 miles from the Lake. Across the street was a motel, so they checked in.

November 27, 1993.
11:30 a.m.

After the four hour ride, Rebecca and Franky were glad to get out of the bus and stretch. They both enjoyed the ride. Even though it was a cloudy, murky day, they caught some beautiful views of the surrounding mountain passes along the drive. They called for a cab, and headed for Rt 167, which ran along the north side of Mono Lake.

Franky thought that the cabby from Sutter Creek was right. As they drove, not one house could be found. The area was barren of people. "Where ya headed?" the cabby asked.

"Well, I don't really know. I'm looking for an old friend

of mine that lives along the Lake, near Rt 167," Franky answered.

"Oh yeah? What's his name?" the cabby asked as he looked at Franky through the rear view mirror.

"Troy Bolger, he moved out here about two years ago."

"Troy! Sure, I know him!" answered the cabby.

"Can you take us to his house?" Franky said excitedly.

"Sure! He's kind of a loner, like most people out here. A couple of times a year he needs to get to the bus station. Other than that, he sticks to himself. Does he know you're coming?"

"Not exactly," Franky answered.

Through the rear view mirror, the cabby looked over Rebecca and Franky apparently in thought. "You say you were friends with Troy?"

"Yeah, kinda," Franky responded.

"Well, I probably would have sent him a letter first or something. You know when I say loner, I mean like he gives the mailman dirty looks."

Franky sat back in the seat and glanced at Rebecca. "This isn't going so well, is it?" he asked softly to her. Rebecca could only nod her head.

"Look. Maybe the guy's looking for shuffleboard partners or something, but I figured I'd just let you know what you're dealing with," the cabby added.

It wasn't long before they pulled off the main road, and onto a single lane dirt road. They drove deeper and deeper into the forest. Franky's stomach turned with anxiety with every mile. Rebecca couldn't talk. She was past fear. Ahead the trees thinned out as Mono Lake appeared before them. To the left was a wood cabin. No telephone lines ran to the house, and no other structures could be seen, except for a small pier and row boat next to the house at the edge of the water. The cab stopped and Franky paid the cabby and exited.

Rebecca and Franky slowly walked in the direction of the house as the cab turned around and drove back. They passed a sign that read: 'Trespassers will be handled with deadly force.'

They stepped up on to the porch just as the door opened halfway and a bearded man in his twenties leaned out the doorway holding a shot gun. "Can't you read, boy?" he asked.

Franky's and Rebecca's eyes popped open wide as they stepped back. "Look, there's no need for that!" Franky said staring at the gun. "I'm an old friend."

"Old friend? You don't look like a friend of mine," he said.

"Are you Troy Bolger?" Franky asked.

"Yeah, who are you?" Troy asked.

"Franky. Franky Carter. This is my wife Rebecca."

"Nope. Don't know a Franky Carter. Now go away," he said closing the door.

"Wait!" Franky yelled as he stepped to the closing door. He had been chased by two guys in suits, shot at, flown 3000 miles, taken a bus and several cabs, just to find Troy Bolger; he wasn't about to just walk away. "We met on Fathom Sound!"

"Never heard of that either! I said go away!" Troy yelled through the closed door.

"You told me on Fathom Sound that your dad took you up in UH-1 helicopters. You explained the instrument panel to me, remember?" Franky screamed.

"So that's it, my dad sent you! If he was a man, he'd have come out here himself! This is the last time I'm going to warn you to leave. Get lost!"

"It was the aliens. The aliens took us to Fathom Sound and taught us Devout Reality. They would abduct us from our bedrooms at night when we were real young!" Franky continued to scream.

This time, Franky got no response from Troy. A few seconds went by that seemed more like hours, then suddenly the door slowly cracked open. Troy peaked out at the two strangers. "Aliens?"

"They use to abduct me, almost every night it seemed. I was so scared of them. Please, I know you don't remember me Troy, but my wife and I are desperate, we need your help," Franky pleaded.

"Come on in," Troy said as the door swung open.

Stunned, they glanced at each other, surprised at Troy's sudden change of heart. They both wondered if entering was a safe thing to do. Slowly, Franky and Rebecca stepped into the small single roomed cabin. Over a raging fire hung a griddle where it was obvious a fish was being cooked as the cabin was filled with its odor. There was no electricity available at the cabin, as burned out candles were sitting in various locations around the room. There was no sign of a electric generator or even battery operated items, such as a radio or television.

"Something smells good," Rebecca said trying to reduce the tension in the room.

"Trout," Troy grumbled.

They sat down around a wooden table next to the fire. Although it was not very cold, the fire helped lessen the chill of the damp air outside. "You mentioned something about aliens?" Troy asked looking at Franky with a cold stare.

"Yeah. When I was child, I'd have these dreams that these skinny, whitish, greyish, creatures with big dark eyes would get me at night, and do an examination on me. At one point in my life, I had these dreams every night. Recently, I underwent hypnosis. This brought back memories of what happened after I was abducted by the aliens as a child. That's when your name came up. During one of my hypnosis sessions, I revealed that you and I were friends on an island called Fathom Sound, which is on another planet. While there, we and a large group of students mostly our same age, learned something called Devout Reality."

"Devout Reality?" Troy said slowly.

"It's an alien science and religion all mixed into one," Franky answered. "Each student had one human instructor assigned to them. My instructor was named Emily, yours was Nathan. At the end of the lessons, I asked you to walk me down along the beach away from the group of students and instructors. Then I ran into the forest in an effort to effect my memory so I could remember all of the events on Fathom Sound, including the people there, like you. As I stepped into the forest that night, you yelled to me and asked that if my plan worked, 'to look you up.' You told me your last name and that you lived in Sacramento. I also knew that your dad was in the military. When we arrived in Sacramento, I met your dad, and he told us that you could be found up here, and so here we are!"

"Hmmm," Troy said as he scratched under his beard while looking over Franky. "Nope. I don't remember you, nor this place you call Fathom Sound."

Franky's hopes died as did his expression of optimism. Rebecca carefully glanced over toward the shot gun sitting next to Troy. She wondered how they would react if Troy became hostile. Franky was just about to apologize for his intrusion, and say good-bye when Troy reached over to his shotgun and placed it on his lap.

"You know," Troy said as he aimed down the barrel of his weapon. ". . .if you had told this same story to anyone of these people who live on this lake, you'd be dead right now."

Rebecca's eyes lit up as she eyeballed the front door. Franky could only stare at the gun.

"So, I guess you must believe what you're saying is true," Troy continued as he cocked open the shot gun and removed the two shells of ammunition.   Franky and Rebecca breathed a deep sign of relief with the unloading of the gun   .

"That fact is, I don't remember anything about Fathom Sound, nor do I remember meeting any Nathan. But, I am an abductee. And no one, and I mean no one, knows that, except it would appear - you." At which time Troy stood up and walked over to a large bookshelf, selected several books and poured them on the wooden table that they sat around. The subject of every book was on either ufos, US cover ups of ufos and aliens, or alien abductions.   "I remember the same dreams you are referring to as a child. I remember the examinations, but that's where my memory stops," Troy said as Franky and Rebecca sorted through the various books.

"There's one more thing about this whole story that's very scary," Franky said as he leafed through one of the books on US government cover-up's of ufos.   "The government's after me. They shot at me and my wife, and they killed my psychiatrist," he said as again some tears filled in Rebecca's eyes.

"The government?" Troy said with a questioning stare. "How do you know it was the government?"

"Government, military. I'm not really sure, but they

bugged the office of my psychiatrist, and now suddenly it's me who is taking the rap for the killing. So we're kind of on the run."

"Why would the government or military want to kill you?" Troy asked.

"I remembered too much. I remembered physics theories about the universe that were taught on Fathom Sound. These theories don't currently exist in the science field, so I guess they felt threatened. Maybe they thought I could prove that ufos are real, and that the government is covering up the whole thing. That's the only thing that makes sense."

"You're not talking about the government then. If what you are saying is true, then you're talking about the military. I'd be the last person to stick up for the government, but what you are saying is just not their work at all. Neither the F.B.I. nor the C.I.A. would be involved in this kind of operation, and neither would any politician. The governments got rules and regulations, and people to report to when things go wrong, and killing a US citizen is kind of messy, even for a politician. No, you're in big time trouble. It's not the government that's after you, you've got a black bag after you," Troy said matter of fact.

"A black bag?" he said confused.

"Yeah, my dad is a liaison to a black bag in Nevada," Troy said.

"It's the military then," Rebecca interrupted.

"Not exactly," answered Troy, ". . .it's a group of personnel who are selected from various branches of the military and science community, to work on super secret programs. Some of the members of black bags are given new names, social security numbers and their former life vanishes. The programs they work on are so secret that even the President of the United States does not have access. The scary thing is that in some cases there are black bags within black bags, where members of the outside black bag don't know what is going on in the inside black bag. It's all in an effort to keep program secrets, secret."

"Where do they get the money to operate?" Rebecca asked.

"Congress," Troy answered.

"Congress knows they exist?" she asked.

"Yeah. Everyone knows they exist, they just don't know what they're doing, or building, or experimenting on. The Stealth Fighter is an example. That was the plane used in the Gulf War. It can hide from enemy radar. It was a black program that was turned over to the Air Force after it was complete. Congress votes to give the black bags billions of dollars every year, fully knowing that they will not know how that money is being spent. Of course, congress expects to occasionally see some product down the line, like the stealth fighter."

"So why would they be after me?" Franky asked.

"Well, if you read the book in your hand, you might have a good idea. According to the book, President Truman created the first black bag and turned the Roswell incident over to it. Since then, only President Eisenhower, knew what happened at Roswell. No congressmen, or even most military generals for that matter have had access to ufo research and data. Whatever is going on with ufos may be known, but not by the government, not by the FBI, CIA, or even most in the military. It's only known by the shadowy black bags within other black bags that operate inside certain military bases."

"So your dad is a liaison to one of these black bags?" Franky asked.

"Yeah, my dad is an Air Force Colonel based at Nellis.

I don't think he really knows specifically what goes on inside the primary black bags. He just delivers products out of the projects or into the projects, and handles two way request either from the Air Force to the black bag or visa versa."

Franky looked down, obviously disappointed. "I was kind of hoping that your dad could get me out of the mess I'm in," Franky said.

"That's what I'm trying to tell you. You are in big time trouble, and I honestly don't know how you can get out of it. If they have decided to take you out, there's no stopping them, and there ain't anyone who can protect you from a group that does not exist. I'm sorry," Troy said sincerely.

Franky looked over at Rebecca terrified, and shook his head in frustration and fear.

"Who else, besides my dad, did you tell you were coming here?" Troy asked.

"No one. Well, besides the cab driver," Franky answered.

"Well, listen, you guys are welcome to stay here a few days, until you figure out what you're going to do, okay?" Troy said.

Franky managed a smile, "Thank you, Troy." But Franky already knew what he had to do. He had to turn himself in. If he didn't, he knew they'd probably kill Rebecca getting to him. It was the information in his head they wanted buried, and the only way to do that was to bury Franky, and now he knew that there was no stopping them.

Chapter Twelve

Area 51

"Consider what would happen if you gave Christopher Columbus a modern nuclear submarine in 1492, and said, 'Chris, money is no object. Build me three more of these babies.' A mighty tall order - and not just because nuclear power was unknown. The internal combustion engine was unknown. Even the steam engine was more than 200 years in the future. The scientific principles governing the skin of the ship, its propulsion, its power source, and its instrumentation did not exist in his world. Even the vessel's purpose might be suspect. Travel below the waves? Why?"

> -Stanton T. Friedman (Nuclear Physicist),
> on reverse-engineering extraterrestrial wreckage
> *"Top Secret / Majic"*

November 28, 1993.
9:30 a.m.

$\mathbb{T}$he two sat quietly in the row boat, somewhere on Mono Lake. The sun had just burned through the morning fog. Troy had to get the night's dinner, and probably still didn't trust Franky and Rebecca enough to leave them both back at the cabin alone, so he asked Franky to go fishing with him. Franky only wished the fishing trip was under better circumstances. The previous night left Franky exhausted since he could not sleep as he pondered his fate.

"What do ya do?" Troy asked as he casted his line.

"Huh?" Franky said glancing over to Troy.

"For a living, What do you do?" Troy clarified.

"Oh. I'm a flight instructor, my wife's a chemical engineer. We live in New Jersey," Franky said.

"Oh yeah. What school did you guys go to?"

"We both went to Florida Tech."

"I'm a Cal Tech boy myself."

Franky looked at Troy surprised. "What, did you think I was some sort of reject or something?" Troy asked noticing Franky's eyebrows rise.

"No. No, you just don't strike me as the college type," Franky said awkwardly.

"Well, what exactly is the college type?" Troy asked.

"I'm sorry. I don't know."

"You think I'm a loafer being out here in the middle of nowhere, don't you?"

"No. I haven't passed any judgement on you," Franky said as he cast his line.

"Dad brought me up to be a soldier. He wanted me to follow in his foot steps, like my brothers did, and I wanted to be a doctor. He let me go to Cal Tech, but demanded that I join the R.O.T.C. Well basically, I'm AWOL from the military and my dad has disowned me," Troy said.

"Your brothers are in the military too?" Franky said surprised.

"Yeah, my family tree is full of soldiers, and Captains, and Colonels, and Majors, and so on and so fourth," Troy said.

"Except you," Franky said looking at him.

"Don't want any part of it."

"So why didn't you just go ahead and become a doctor?"

"After graduation I had to fulfill my military obligation with the R.O.T.C. before I could go on to medical school. That's when I went A.W.O.L. I lived with a few friends at first, then found this place out here for sale, bought it, and now here I am. You can't beat it either," Troy said as he cast his line into the water angrily.

"I'm going to turn myself in," Franky said looking down at his feet.

"What?" Troy said surprised, "Did you kill anyone?"

"No, but if I don't, they'll eventually find me, and when they do they'll have to kill Rebecca too."

"There's gotta be another way."

The two sat fishing in silence for the next half hour, trying to come up with a solution. "Nothing biting today," Troy finally said.

"Is it true that there are 400 billion stars in our galaxy?"

Franky asked.

"Yeah, that's what they have calculated."

"And that there are another 80 billion galaxies, each with hundreds of billions of stars?"

"Yep!"

"And that the average star has 6 to 9 planets around it?"

"Mm-hm," Troy said looking over at Franky.

"That's a big universe," Franky concluded remembering the statistics from one of Troy's books the night before.

"Hard to imagine, huh?"

"The universe has got to be churning with life," Franky said as he looked up into the hazy sky. "I wish Emily could help me now."

"So we were on an island together, huh?" Troy said as he looked around the lake.

"Fathom Sound, it's called. And to be technical, we really were never there."

"What?" Troy said raising his voice.

"Well, it's kind of complicated, but when we were conceived, the aliens took a genetic duplicate of our DNA make-up and created another one of us, a clone. The clone was brought to full term in an alien environment. So there is another Franky and another Troy, exactly like us. They learned on Fathom Sound with our memories and those memories were later transplanted into our heads during an abduction. So technically our physical bodies were never off this planet, just our memories were; our minds so to speak."

"What is this Devout Reality?" Troy asked.

"Basically, to give. When conscious beings give as a social whole to one another, on a giant scale, and without exception, nature around that social whole begins to change. Things just seem to start occurring beneficially for the entire Social Order. Finally, the climax of such a process is called a Collective Inception, that's when nature is so radically changed that even the weather and wild animals behave oddly. Clouds will form into squares, and animals may march in perfect sync with one another."

"So the aliens want us to start this process here on Earth?" Troy asked.

"Yeah, they've even altered our genetic make-up to do it. They say that emotions like pride, greed and vengeance prohibit the giving process, so they have begun to remove those emotions from human nature."

"So that's why they're here. Do you know the extent of government assistance to the aliens?" asked Troy.

"The aliens need no assistance. They only need those who know about their presence to remain silent. I was told that the US government recovered one of their ships in New Mexico. It was taken to an Air Force base. The aliens later met with the military and worked some kind of deal out. They asked the military for its help to keep the alien's presence on Earth a secret. The agreement made was called, The Dreamland Alliance."

"Dreamland?" Troy interrupted, "That's Area 51. That's at Nellis Air Force Test Range, which is only 100 miles southeast of here."

"I heard. They called it S-4. That's probably where they meet," Franky said as he cast another line.

"Meet?" Troy said.

"Yeah, the Alliance stipulates that the aliens must meet with the military every ten years to release some technology, in exchange for the military's promise to keep the alien operation a secret," Franky said.

"I can see why they'd want you dead!"

Suddenly Franky's line snapped tight as his pole bent

into the water. "You got one!" Troy yelled.

After a little struggle, Franky cranked the nine pound bass into the boat. For the first time in days, Franky smiled. "Will this do for dinner?" he asked.

"Oh yeah! Easy," Troy answered with a smile of his own.

"You didn't happen to catch a date did you?" Troy asked.

"A date?"

"When they meet - the aliens and the black bag."

"They said every ten years starting on December 23rd, 1963," Franky said as he sized up the bass.

Troy stopped what he was doing, and stared at Franky. Franky spotted Troy's glare, "What?" Franky asked.

"1963? Don't you see the significance of that?" Troy asked.

"No, what?"

"63, 73, 83 . . ." Troy said slowly.

"93!" Franky said as his eyes lit up. "December 23rd, 1993!"

"Exactly!" Troy said excitedly. "That gives us a little more than 3 weeks before the next meeting!"

"Yeah. But how does that help me?" Franky asked.

"I'm not sure, but if we can figure out how to get you in there during the meeting, maybe, just maybe our little grey friends could help you!"

"But how are we supposed to get in there?" Franky asked.

"December 23rd, hmm," Troy said as he glared out on the lake. "That date makes perfect sense. It would give the black bag an excuse to clear Nellis of most personnel. Most personnel would be released for the Christmas holiday, and I'd imagine the only people that remain would be those involved in the Dreamland Alliance.

"There's no way of walking across. The desert is guarded with infra-red cameras that can spot a rodent half a mile away. Can't drive through, even if we somehow got my dads id card, that wouldn't be realistic. . ."

"I know!" Franky yelled as he stood up on the boat excitedly. "I know how! We'll fly in! I've got a plane back in Sutter Creek! We'll just fly in and land as the meeting is going on!" Franky said with a smile.

"Sit back down," Troy said seriously. "They'd knock you out of the sky faster than you can say Carl Lewis."

"Oh. But, what if I flew low to the ground, couldn't I avoid radar that way?" Franky asked as he sat down.

"Yeah, maybe if you we're trying to enter the Canadian border, but no way are you going to be able to get under the Nellis Air Force Base radar, no way!"

Franky sat there thinking a moment when another idea struck him, "What about through the radar?"

"What?"

"What if I fly through the radar without an airplane around me? Would the radar pick me up then?" Franky asked.

"What are you going to do, hire superman?" Troy asked with a laugh.

"No seriously, would I avoid the radar then?"

"Yeah, but how ya going to do that?"

"Back in Jersey, I've got a glider with a fabric body. What if I glided all the way into the Test Range?"

"That's an interesting idea. I'm not really sure if it could work or not. Does the glider have instruments? Like an altimeter, gyroscope, or radio?"

"Yeah."

"Well, if it could work, we'd have to remove those

instruments, then maybe, just maybe it might work. Radar waves bounce off of anything solid, but, if we get rid of some of that hardware, you might be mistaken for ground clutter, humidity, or even birds. It'd be very risky, though. Even if it could work, how would you get it here from Jersey?"

"I have a friend who I might be able to get to help me. Do you know where I can get to a phone?" Franky asked as they began to row back to the cabin.

They rowed back to the cabin in silence, each wondering how feasible was the plan.

"We've got a plan!" Franky yelled to Rebecca as they opened the cabin door. "It's a long shot, but it's better than nothing," he added. Franky and Troy explained the plan to Rebecca and then told her that they were going to walk out to the main road where there was a pay phone. Rebecca had been reading through a variety of Troy's books, and decided to prepare the fish while they were gone.

They walked down the long dirt road with a pace of excitement. They had a plan, one that had many problems. Would they be able to avoid radar, even without many of the instruments on board, and then would Franky be able to fly the glider without those same instruments. Even if he did make it to Area 51, would there be aliens? What if the date had been changed? And even if they did get the date right, at what time should he make the attempt? Despite all these very real problems, Franky was excited. He went from turning himself over to a death squad, to hope, regardless of how slim the chances for survival.

"You eat anything besides fish?" Franky asked.

"No, that's the only thing I eat," Troy said with a sarcastic sound to his voice, "Of course I eat other things. I eat deer, I have a garden, and I go to town for long term supplies of oat and grain, and cereals."

"Just wondering," Franky said defensively.

"How far can one of those gliders go?" Troy asked.

"Depends on the weather and geological conditions, but on average about ten miles of ground distance to every 1000 feet of altitude."

"So if you were coming in at 10,000 feet, you could glide about 100 miles?" Troy asked.

"On average."

"What do you do to get up to the 10,000 feet? What are you towed by a plane?"

"Yeah," Franky answered.

"Well then, you're gonna need that 100 miles of gliding. Area 51's radar will be all over that plane towing the glider, and you don't want any attention drawn in your vicinity. If they think something is up, they'll concentrate their radar in on that sector, and even the glider will be nailed. You better stretch the glide out as long as you can, maybe get released at 15,000 feet or something."

They arrived to the main road and began to walk a short way until they reached a pay phone at the side of the road. Franky pulled out his calling card and began to dial. He was surprised to see that it was still activated. "I guess they didn't get to the calling card," Franky said as he hoped for Bob-O to answer his home phone.

"Hello?" Bob-O answered.

"Bob-O! It's Franky!"

"Franky! Where have you been? You got the whole world out looking for you!" Bob-O yelled into the phone.

"I need your help," Franky started.

"You need more than my help, Franky!" Bob-O replied.

"Listen to me, I don't care what anyone is saying. I did not kill Dr. Skye!"

"Then why are you on the run?"

"It's all very complicated and hard to explain right now, but I need you to just trust me."

"Look Franky, I don't know what you have in mind, but if I help you do anything, I might end up in jail myself," Bob-O said.

"It's not jail I'm afraid of. Two guys were trying to kill me, and killed Dr. Skye, and they've been chasing me ever since! Now, you've known Rebecca and I for how many years? Five? You know that I could never kill an insect let alone a human being!"

"I know! I know! That's what just doesn't make any sense. That's exactly what everyone's been talking about. How you could ever do something like that. But then, why did you runaway?"

"I told you! These two guys are after me! Didn't you see the fence at the airport? They drove right through it trying to get to me."

"But why didn't you just go to the police instead of the airport?"

"The people trying to kill me are part of a faction of the government. It's too difficult to explain right now, but we need your help. In fact, our lives depend on it!"

Franky and Bob-O were best friends. Bob-O was Franky's best man, and he was the type of person who would do anything for you. This seemed extremely unusual, but Bob-O was a loyal friend. "Okay, what is it?"

"You're still going home for Christmas, right. You're flying your twin to Texas, right?" Franky asked.

"Yeah, so?"

"I need you to make a detour on your way."

"A detour?"

"I'm going to fly the Cessna back to the Red Lion, we'll

hook up the glider to your twin, then I need you to take me to California."

"What? That's some detour! And if you show your face around here, the F.B.I. will be more than happy to give you a change of scenery."

"That's why we'll met at the airport at like 3 am or something. We'll hook up and off we'll go."

Bob-O paused, "What night?" he finally said slowly.

"Thank you, we owe our lives to you! How about December 2nd, 3 am?"

Bob-O agreed. After they hung up, they headed back toward the cabin. "So you're going to have to fly back to Jersey?" Troy asked.

"If I want that glider I'm gonna have to. I'm gonna have to leave tomorrow," Franky responded.

"I'm gonna leave with you," Troy said.

Franky looked over at Troy surprised, "No, no, it may be dangerous. In fact, I was going to ask you if it would be okay if Rebecca stayed at the cabin."

"That's fine, but you don't understand what I was going to say. I'm going to head back to Sutter Creek with you. I'm gonna stay a few days with my dad."

"What for? Won't he have you arrested for being A.W.O.L?"

"No. But maybe I can get some information from him, like about the 23rd. If this kind of thing happens every ten years, I'm sure he knows that something is going on there, maybe not UFO's but I'm sure he's aware that there is going to be some sort of black bag experiment, the key thing is to get the time of the event, if he even knows it, I'll get it out of him. If I can do that, maybe you have a shot at this whole thing."

Franky smiled and put his hand on Troy's shoulder. "I

knew you were all right!"

They stepped into the cabin in laughter. Rebecca had just finished putting the fish onto the grill over the fire, when they entered the cabin. "What's so funny?" she asked smiling herself now.

"I was just telling him about how we scrambled to get out of Jersey, it was like a James Bond film or something. Which brings up another point, I gotta go back to Red Lion to get the glider."

"Why!" Rebecca said as her smile turned to a frown, "We'll be killed! Can't Bob-O bring the glider here?"

"No! You need a pilot in the tow plane, and in the glider at the same time. Plus, I need to return the Cessna back to Red Lion. And I want you to stay here at the cabin. Okay?"

"No, I'm not staying here, no way!"

"It's the only way. Your extra weight on the plane is going to slow us down. It's bad enough that Bob-O's twin is going to be pulling a glider. Any extra weight we want to avoid," Franky quickly pointed out. Even though what he was saying was partially true, the main reason for his objection was Rebecca's safety. He knew that the trip could end in disaster if he was spotted.

That night, as they all slept, the air outside grew turbulent. "What's that noise?" Franky wondered half awake. A low rumble grew in intensity as the trees outside began to sway. Franky quickly opened his eyes to find the entire cabin lit up brightly, as the thunderous roar outside became deafening. Troy quickly ran across to Rebecca and Franky and stood them up. He then rolled up a throw rug, and opened a wooden hinged door on the floor. He yelled to them to get down inside and to be quiet. They did so.

Troy then closed the hatch, and covered it back up with

the carpet, and laid back down on his bed. A sudden explosion at the door pushed open the cabin door as a group of men dressed in black uniforms and helmets, burst inside. Troy leaped up out of bed with eyes open wide. A man in the center took off his helmet, and stepped toward Troy.

"We're looking for two murderers who were seen in this area," he yelled over the helicopter engines that were hovering outside and providing the light. "Have you seen anyone? One male, and one female!"

Troy shook his head, "No! Now get off my property!" he yelled.

The man then stepped to Troy face to face and stared into his eyes. "Don't tell me what to do, boy! I'll tell you what to do! Do you understand?"

Troy again shook his head.

"Search the place!" he yelled to his men. The team immediately scattered through the cabin, turning over furniture, knocking over his bed, and checking the bathroom. A bead of sweat ran down Troy's head as he glanced down at the carpet concealing Rebecca and Franky.

"It's empty sir," one said to the man who then put his helmet back on.

"This never happened, okay?" he snarled at Troy.

"No problem," Troy quickly responded.

The man then turned around as if he was about to leave, stopped suddenly, then wheeled back around again toward Troy, punching him in the jaw and knocking him to the floor. "Tell anyone about this, and we'll be back!" he said as he left.

After Troy was sure they were gone, he quickly rolled up the rug, and opened the hatch, letting Rebecca and Franky out. "So that's where you keep your oats and grains for the winter!" Franky said.

Troy lit a candle, which exposed the bruise to his face. "What happened!" Rebecca asked.

"That son of bitch cheap shoted me!"

Franky looked down at the floor. "I'm sorry. This is all my fault. Now I've gotten you in danger, too."

Troy walked over to him, "Listen, we're in this together now. So stop feeling sorry for yourself, and let's get going."

"What?" Franky said surprised.

"If they know you're here, they probably know about your plane in Sutter Creek. You're gonna have to take the plane by surprise, I'd bet they have a couple of guys watching it night and day. But if you tried to get it at night, you might have a chance to get up in the air."

Rebecca and Franky hugged and said 'good-bye.' Troy and Franky then made their way through the forest, avoiding the main dirt road, toward the pay phone. Troy and Franky theorized that the use of Franky's calling card attracted the black project to the area. After contacting a cab, they waited in the trees along the road. After reaching the bus terminal they boarded the bus for Sutter Creek.

November 30, 1993.
2:00 a.m.

Troy had the cab driver let them out about a mile away from the airport. They stepped away from the cab. "Can you make it from here?" asked Troy. "If you stay off the road, you'll bring less attention to yourself."

"Yeah, I should be all right. I'll see you back at the cabin in about week?" Franky said.

"Yep. Good luck."

Franky snuck up to the airport fence, and climbed over top. He then crawled his way to his plane. He couldn't see

anyone around at all. Quickly he started the plane and
rolled out to the runway within seconds. As he took off, he
could see headlights of a car go on, in the airport parking
lot. "Did they miss me?" Franky wondered to himself.

December 2, 1993.
3:00 a.m.

Franky's Cessna touched down on the Red Lion runway,
and as he pulled up to the parking ramp, he could see that
Bob-O was standing next to his twin. Franky parked and
shut down the tired engine.

"Thanks for doing this Bob-O. I owe you big time!"

"You bet you do!" Bob-O said as he shook his friends
hand firmly.

Franky carefully looked around the airport hoping not to
see any unusual cars. The fence was still damaged. "When
they gonna fix that?" Franky asked pointing at the gapping
hole in the fence.

"This place? Probably never," Bob-O chuckled.

Franky lined the black glider up on the runway, while
Bob-O started his twin engine Duchess. Slowly, Bob-O
rolled the twin in position just in front of the glider. Franky
snapped a cable that connected the glider to the tail of the
twin, then signaled Bob-O that the connection was made.
Once Franky secured himself in the glider, the two 180
horse power engines of the Duchess fired up to maximum
power. The thrust jolted Franky into his gliders seat as the
two crafts quickly reached take-off speed.

This time, the trip seemed to take much longer. Sitting
alone in the glider with nothing to do but occasionally make
slight adjustments to the planes guidance, made the trip
seem more tiresome. When they stopped to sleep, Franky

explained the entire story. Everything from his youthful abductions, to Emily, to his plan to glide into Area 51. Despite Bob-O's attempt to get Franky to change his mind, he finally agreed to pilot the towing plane on the night Franky was going to make the attempted glide. Since Franky and the glider would be released far from Area 51, Bob-O would be in no danger.

December 5, 1993.
11:00 p.m.

They touched down on the Hawthorne Municipal Airport runway in Hawthorne, Nevada. Not a minute too soon either. Franky was now completely exhausted from the three trans-continental flights in less than a month that he had flown. They wheeled the glider to a parking ramp where ultalights, and other light aircraft, were parked, and tied it down. They also parked the twin Duchess.

Hawthorne Municipal Airport was closer to Mono Lake than Sutter Creek, and Franky did not want to return to Sutter Creek for fear of being detected by the black project agents. This airport was only across the border from California, about sixty miles northeast of Mono Lake. The next day, they figured they would catch a bus.

Bob-O told his parents in Texas that he would be arriving on the 24th. He figured if he released Franky on the 23rd, then went directly to Texas, he'd arrive home by 3:00 p.m. on the 24th. Bob-O of course had serious reservations about believing Franky's story. It all seemed impossible. However, no matter how strange it seemed, he was his best friend, and he had promised to go through with this crazy stunt.

December 6, 1993.
7:30 p.m.

Rebecca and Troy had begun to grow worried about Franky. They debated how long it would take for Franky to get back. In the midst of the debate, Franky opened the door. Rebecca instantaneously leaped up and ran to him. Without saying a word, they hugged, as she began to cry.

"Hey Rebecca! Nice seeing you too!" Bob-O said sarcastically as he stepped into the cabin.

"I'm sorry Bob-O. Give me a hug!" she said as she stepped over to him with open arms.

"Bob-O, this is Troy, Troy Bolger," Franky said as Troy stood up and extended a hand to Bob-O.

"I've heard a lot about you the last couple of days, and to be honest, until right this minute I wasn't sure if you were only a figment of Franky's imagination," Bob-O said with a laugh.

Troy just laughed, as they all gathered around the wooden table. Troy and Franky had to sit on the bed, since there was a shortage of chairs. "I'm sorry, I don't usually have guests over," Troy commented.

"How did it go at home?" Franky asked Troy.

"Interesting. Dad yelled, and I just took it. And then he yelled some more, like I was a teenager or something. I stayed there for four days, and just said that I wanted to see everyone for the holidays. I never mentioned work with my dad, until the last day. I figured it wouldn't be as suspicious. I said that I was thinking of coming home on the 23rd for Christmas, and wanted to know if he would be home. He said that he wouldn't until early on the 24th. I then asked him why so late this year. He said that there was a base Christmas party being held on December 23rd, after dinner. I asked if mom was going, and he said that it was for military personnel only. Mom always goes to these kind of things. This must be it."

"I tried to pin him down to a time, but he wouldn't give in. The best I could do was late on the 23rd. I'd imagine well after sunset," Troy concluded.

"That's a big help. I know going back home was the last thing you wanted."

"Tomorrow, Bob-O and I are going to go back to the airport, in Hawthorne, Nevada. Bob-O's gonna rent a car for us to use, and we're going to start modifying the glider by taking out the altimeter, gyroscopes, and radios. The only thing we're going to leave in the glider is an airspeed indicator. Do you think that will hurt us, Troy?" Franky asked.

"I don't know. I don't even know if this is going to work at all. I would just recommend taking out as much as you can."

"Do you want to go with us, Troy," Franky asked.

"I guess so."

"What about me? I'm tired of staying here alone. No offense Troy, but do you guys have any idea how boring it is here?" Rebecca said raising her voice.

"You can go too!" Franky said smiling.

The next day, they took a bus out to Hawthorne Municipal Airport. Just across the street was a Hertz Rental. Bob-O rented a four door Ford Escort, and drove it across the street to the glider. They spent much of the day removing what they could from it. Franky figured he could manage to control the glider with just the airspeed indicator. After reaching 14,000 feet, he would be released about 100 miles northwest of the center of the Nellis Air Force Range. If he maintained 70 knots on the airspeed indicator, he would make it to the center and still have about 2000 feet of altitude to find Area 51.

That night, they stayed at a motel in downtown Hawthorne. They bought a map of Nevada and spread it out on the motel bed.

Bob-O circled a spot on the map, "Right here. This is about 100 miles northwest of the range. That would put us above Mina, Nevada."

"Mina! What? That's only about ten miles from here! How you gonna get to 14,000 feet in ten miles? Is that possible?" Troy asked.

"Well, I guess we'll have to do a lot of climbing circles," Franky said.

"I want to go!" Rebecca said with a very serious tone to her voice.

"No! No way. You're not going anywhere!" Franky snapped.

"Look, you're my husband, and I want to go with you. Whatever happens, I'm willing to pay the consequences!" she said.

"Well, I'm not!" Franky said sternly.

"You can go with me!" Bob-O yelled. "You can ride up with me in the Duchess. Franky's right, Rebecca."

"Franky's right, Rebecca," Troy added. "It's too risky. Besides, two people in that glider is only going to add to the radar signature. You might cause both of your deaths by going!"

"Okay, but I at least want to go up with Bob-O," she said reluctantly.

"Hell, I'm not going to be the only one sitting down on the ground, you better leave a seat in twin open for me too!" Troy said.

"I guess it's a send off party," Bob-O said with a smile.

Rebecca refused to smile though. The danger of the mission was starting to sink in. For the first time, she realized that if it failed, she would never again see her husband.

Chapter Thirteen

Touchdown

"Courage is resistance to fear, mastery of fear, not absence of fear."

-Mark Twain

December 23, 1993.
8:00 p.m.

Rebecca and Franky kissed in the cool night air on the airport ramp. "I love you," she said with tears running down her cheeks.

"I love you too," he said. "If I don't . . ."

Quickly Rebecca put her hand to his mouth, "You will!" she said. "I will see you again!" she cried.

"After you guys release me, get out of here! Okay?" Franky said to Rebecca.

Rebecca could only nod.

"We better get this thing started," Bob-O said as he walked up to them.

"Anybody see any stars moving up there?" Franky said causing a few uncomfortable laughs.

Troy and Bob-O jumped into the front two seats of the Duchess, while Rebecca climbed into the backseat, never releasing her stare on Franky. Franky closed the glass canopy of the glider, enclosing him inside. As the engines of the Duchess roared to life, Franky's heart began to pound in his throat.

Inside the Duchess, no one could speak, their mouths were too dry. Bob-O put his sweaty hands on the throttle and powered the twin and glider into position on the runway. Rebecca plastered her face to the back window of the twin trying to make eye contact with Franky, who was positioned behind them. Bob-O applied full throttle, causing the tow cable between the aircraft to become tight. As the Duchess lifted off the ground, Bob-O detracted it's landing gear.

Steadily, they climbed directly over the airport until reaching 14,000 feet. When the Duchess banked out of the steady turns and leveled off, Franky knew they had reached 14,000 feet. "This is it!" he said to himself. Bob-O told Franky that he would turn the Duchess' navigation lights off when they were over Mina. That would be the cue to release himself from the twin, and begin his 70 knot descent toward the center of the base. In Franky's sweaty palm, he clutched a glow in the dark magnetic compass. With it, he could direct the glider to the southeast 135 degrees.

The Duchess began its straight and level course toward a group of lights laying on the surface below. Franky knew that the approaching lights were that of the city of Mina. Rebecca cried aloud in the back seat. "No! No! Why can't we just hide at the lake? He's going to die! No! We have to turn around!" she screamed.

Bob-O turned to Rebecca and put his hand on her shoulder, "We've come too far."

Troy looked over to Bob-O, "That's Mina below us, isn't it?"

"Yeah," Bob-O said with a trembling voice.

Rebecca turned back toward the glider and screamed through the back window, "No! Franky! Don't do it!"

Troy could only stare at Bob-O's shaking hand as he reached for the switch that turned off the planes navigation lights. "God help him," Bob-O said as he flipped the switch.

Franky wiped the sweat from his forehead, as the Duchess' lights went out. Without hesitation, Franky released the glider from the cable that kept it in tow. He banked left to 135 degrees on his compass, and established a 70 knot glide speed. He could not hear his wife's frantic screams as the two aircraft separated.

"Sir, we have a bogey 97 miles about 305 degrees at one four zero feet," the Nellis radar officer said.

"Let me see that," said Colonel Bolger. "Where is that, over Mina?"

"I believe so, sir."

"Okay, keep an eye on that. If it comes in to within 90 miles let me know."

"Sir! Looks like it just turned north!"

"Good," the Colonel sighed.

Franky tried to keep the glider still, knowing that even slight movements of the wings could add to a radar signature. After about fifty minutes, Franky figured he had been successful, even though he had not entered the actual Air Force base airspace. He thought that if they had seen him on radar, they'd be all over him by now.

"Sir! Can you take a look at this?" the radar officer yelled.

"What is it," the Colonel asked as he approached the screen.

"Remember the bogey over Mina?"

"Yes, is it still there?"

"No, but something just kind of showed up between us and Mina!"

"Give me a speed and trajectory," Colonel Bolger snapped.

"Looks like, it's out of eight zero feet at about 74 knots and inbound at one three five degrees."

Colonel Bolger's eyes strained to find the soft radar trace on the screen. "What is that? That's no plane!"

"Uh, I'm not sure, but whatever it is, if it keeps this heading, it'll be right over Area 51!" the radar officer yelled as he suddenly realized the calculations he was figuring.

Colonel Bolger raced over to a telephone in the control room, "Dispatch! This is Colonel Bolger, we have a bogey inbound! He's now at seven five feet, out at 305 degrees northwest of Area 51, presently 68 miles, coming in at 74 knots! I want five Apache's up to check that out, NOW! And Major, you better put up an Eagle till we figure out what this thing is," Colonel Bolger said with stress in his voice.

The Colonel asked for five Apache attack helicopters. Apache's are well armed, high tech, seek and destroy type helicopters. With infra-red night seeing equipment, they surely could find Franky. His body heat alone would give him away from up to a mile away. The Eagle is an F-15 Air Superiority Interceptor Fighter. In case the helicopters couldn't handle the bogey, the Eagle certainly would.

Franky was now within 40 miles of Area 51 and at 4,500 feet. Not a single light on the desert floor below could be seen. The only lights Franky could see were from the stars above. Only the soft wisping wind, skirting the canopy around him, made a sound. Silence prevailed.

With a good visibility, Franky could now see lights in the distances. "Area 51!" he thought. Then, one seemed to move. They were also growing brighter. Three lights directly ahead of him were swaying, "They've found me!" he suddenly realized as the inbound lights quickly approached. Franky briskly looked to the right, and left. In both cases, he saw one more approaching light at the same altitude.

"This is Charlie Charlie Four Zero Niner, we have bogey in sight," one of the Apache pilots said into his headset.

"What is it?" Colonel Bolger yelled.

"Non powered glider, one occupant," the pilot replied.

"Stay with the bogey!" commanded the Colonel. Colonel Bolger picked up another phone and paused.

Answering was a deep southern accented voice, "Red dispatch."

"Red, this is Colonel Bolger, we have a problem. Are you guys in progress?"

"Never mind that, son. What's the problem?" the voice asked.

"We've got somebody in a glider in bound to the test range," Colonel Bolger said nervously.

"How far away is he, Colonel?"

"Just under 30 nautical miles."

"What? Do you have anyone up on him?"

"Yes sir, we have some Apache's and an Eagle!" Colonel Bolger answered.

"Well, what are you waiting for, a landing on the damn runway? Down him!" the voice said as the phone hung up.

Colonel Bolger shook his head slightly. He then hung up the phone, walked over to another phone and picked it up. "Charlie Charlie Four Zero Niner . . ."

"Go base, this is Charlie Charlie Four Zero Niner," the pilot replied.

"Splash the bogey!" Colonel Bolger said clearly.

"Splash him?" the pilot returned.

"You heard me Lieutenant. I want him down, then I want you all back immediately!"

"Roger Charlie Charlie Four Zero Niner understand splash bogey!" said the pilot.

Franky could see that the lights had been keeping a specific distance from him as he continued his approach toward Area 51. In fact, he could now see runway lights in the distance. "How close were they going to let me get?" he wondered. He was just about to get his answer.

"Target locked," the pilot announced as he lifted the firing safety covering a trigger that released an infra-red guided missile. "Fire!" he yelled as he squeezed the firing trigger.

Franky immediately saw a flash brightly light up under one of the helicopters. He knew what that was instantly. They fired on him. The missile streaked directly at him as he attempted to push the glider straight down. The missile was faster than his reflexes and it was apparent that it was going to hit him directly in the cockpit. Franky closed his eyes, knowing he would not feel the pain.

Suddenly, he sank into his seat as G-forces pushed his head back to the seat. The glider was now in a 90 degree angle going straight up into the night air. Franky could hear the crackle of the missile as it passed below him, missing the glider by a few feet. The glider rapidly accelerated, still climbing vertically into the air.

"What?" the pilot said stunned. "I've got a miss!"

Colonel Bolger nearly choked on his coffee when he heard over the intercom that there was a miss. Colonel Bolger picked up the phone, "Miss? Knock him out with your cannon then! Maybe he doesn't have enough signature for you to lock!"

"Sir! You better take a look at this!" the radar officer said interrupting the Colonel.

Colonel Bolger looked at the radar screen as the stunned pilot came over the intercom, "You're not going to believe this sir, but I lost the bogey!"

Colonel Bolger watched the radar screen as the glider's signature indicated that it was shooting through 20,000 feet and still climbing. "Eagle One! You read?" Colonel Bolger yelled into the phone.

"Roger this is Eagle One," the pilot responded.

"You got the bogey?"

"Roger, he's coming up on me, now. Do I understand you want the bogey splashed?"

"Roger! Splash him!" the Colonel yelled.

The F-15 sharply banked in the direction of the glider. Rapidly they approached each other. As they did, the F-15 opened cannon fire, dispersing several rounds of forty millimeter shells in the direction of the glider that now was glowing soft purple.

Franky could not move, as G-forces strained against his body. He could see the bright colored rounds of ammunition around him, as the glider spun and darted to avoid each shell. The glider then continued to move toward the F-15, and accelerated to many times the speed of sound, passing within inches of the Eagle. The Eagle pilot watched helplessly as he temporarily lost control of his jet due to the wake turbulence cast off of the speeding glider.

With his great speed, Franky knew that the fabric wings of his glider should have disintegrated long before now. He looked up through the canopy and spotted the answer. Above him hovered a glowing silver disk. Franky smiled and uncontrollably screamed, "YES!" as he thrusted his fist into the air.

Personnel poured out onto the Area 51's runway as Franky, the glider, and the silver disk, lowered close to the runway surface. The glider gently touched down on the runway surface, and Franky popped the hatch. After undoing his seat belt, he stepped out onto the runway with trembling legs. He turned to look at the personnel, who were all dressed in black, as they approached him.

Someone grabbed Franky by his arm, and pulled him away from his glider.

Tiny lights flickered everywhere around the base which were spread out in a hallow between several mountain ridges. One such ridge laid directly behind the base's hangers and buildings. The silver disk slowly passed over the heads of the group of personnel, then came to stop next to the group, only inches above the ground. A soft glowing purple light lit up the ground directly beneath the silent vessel.

A small section of the ships wall suddenly melted away, exposing a brightly lit interior. Something was pulling Franky toward the door. Then as he looked down, he was shocked to see his legs walking toward the vessel. Franky didn't fight his legs, and walked to the ship's opening. The group around the vessel did nothing but watch. Franky was unsure if that was because they couldn't or that they did not want to interfere.

When he stepped into the ship, he spotted an alien standing to his left. The room was very familiar, being white and oval shaped. The alien was also familiar, its thin frame stood a little higher than five feet. Its color was bright grey. Somehow, Franky knew this was the same alien that abducted him as a child.

The creature reached out to Franky and grabbed his hand. Franky smiled and said, "Hello."

The creature moved its thin mouth slightly, in an apparent attempt to smile. They walked into another room, Franky recognized this room as the control room. The walls around him seemed to disappear, as they could now see the base and all of the personnel gathered around the ship.

"Look to the ridge, and go there. Remember?" the

creature said non-verbally.

"Yes!" Franky said as he stared at the ridge and concentrated. Franky looked at his feet to see the moving pavement below. He was making the ship move! He looked back up toward the ridge, and slowly the craft increased its speed along the ground. As they approached the ridge, the alien lifted one of its thin hands. When it did, a section of the mountain ridge began to move, revealing a dark entrance way into the mountain itself.

Franky noticed some movement to the side of the ship, and as he looked, two other silver vessels could be seen following them into the mountain. Slowly they entered into the mountain. The tunnel angled slightly downward, and as they maneuvered down, light could be seen. As the ship approached the end of the tunnel, Franky's mouth opened wide, stunned at what he was seeing.

A small city constructed under the mountain emerged below them. The entire ridge appeared to be hollowed out. At the center of the city rose three massive pillars, extending from the base of the ridge to the ceiling. Each pillar had thousands of windows, leaving Franky with the notion that the pillars not only provided support, but office, administrative, or residential space. Many large, more traditional buildings existed throughout the cavern, either rising up from its base, or hanging down from the ceiling.

The three silver disks slowly descended to a flat ramp area located in the center of the city. There, three humans dressed in military dress blues stood. Franky recognized one as Colonel Bolger, Troy's dad. The wall melted away, and the alien and Franky exited to greet the humans.

"That was some stunt you played boy!" the one military officer said with a deep southern accent.

"Hello again sir," Franky said to Colonel Bolger.

"You know this boy?" asked the military officer to Colonel Bolger.

"No!" he denied to his superior, "Where do I know you from?" Colonel Bolger asked Franky.

"About a month ago, I asked you where I could find Troy," Franky answered.

"That's right! So, that's why Troy came home and had so much interest in tonight."

"Franky!" the alien said to him non-verbally. Franky looked over to the alien who was pointing toward the other ship. As the door melted away, out ran Rebecca toward Franky. They embraced. He could see Troy and Bob-O and another alien stepping out of the same ship.

"But how did you guys . . ." Franky started.

"They were watching the whole thing! That was some maneuver you put on that F-15!" Bob-O yelled.

"But what about the Duchess?" Franky asked confused.

"It's next to your glider," Bob-O answered with a smile as he looked around the underground city.

"Hi dad," Troy said to his surprised father.

"This is great! How are we supposed to fix this one?" the officer asked looking at Colonel Bolger.

"I'm sorry sir. I had nothing to do with this."

One of the aliens stepped over to Franky and placed its long thin arm on his shoulder, "Over there," it said to him as it pointed toward the third ship.

The wall had already been open. Out stepped a woman and an older man.

"Emily?" Franky said as he took a few steps toward them. She smiled.

Franky was surprised to see that Emily was much older than he remembered. He stepped toward her and hugged her. "You got old!" he said with a laugh.

"And so did you!" she said with an even bigger laugh.

"Hello, Franky," Nathan said.

"Nathan! I thought that was you. This is like a reunion!" Franky exclaimed.

"Seems like your memory has gotten you in some more trouble," Nathan said.

Franky smiled, "Sorry."

Troy walked up behind Franky. "Troy, this is Emily and Nathan, do you remember now?"

"No. I'm sorry, I don't remember you," he said to Nathan.

Then to both of their shock, out stepped Franky's and Troy's clones. They each approached their clone brothers, and extended their hands. "How about me? You remember me," Troy's clone asked him.

"Only in the mirror," he said seriously, amazed to be staring at himself.

Franky stared into the face of his identical clone. Faintly, he began to hear words formulate in his head. "We d- - - - t," he heard in his head.

Franky mouthed silently and thought, "What?".

Then to his surprise, his clone smiled as the words clearly were heard in Franky's head this time, "We did it!" the clone said telepathically.

Franky thought he understood how. Since their brains were identical, and shared memories, they were able to communicate telepathically. "We did what?" Franky asked without speaking.

"You kept your memory," the clone answered.

Franky shook his head and smiled. Then a thought occurred to Franky, "How close to each other do we have to be to communicate with one another?" he asked.

"The cosmic consciousness is everywhere, and is a

timeless, spaceless existence. It therefore is not bound by distance! We've been talking to each other since we were born, Franky!" the clone answered.

Franky's mouth dropped open in disbelief. After a few moments Franky spoke aloud, forgetting that it was not neccessary. "And I thought I was schizophrenic!"

Troy turned to Franky, "What?"

Realizing his mistake, Franky snapped out of his trance, "Nothing, I was just talking to myself - pardon the pun."

"So what now?" Franky asked Emily.

"Well, take a look over in that office," Emily said pointing to a building next to the first ship. Franky could see an alien handing something that resembled a metallic cube to one of the military officers. "They're releasing some computer technology. Your safety is assured. The aliens have told them that if any harm should come to you, the alliance will be dissolved."

"But how did you know to come here? How did you know we were going to try this?" Franky asked.

"We didn't. But when the aliens were approaching the base, they saw you in the glider, and the others in the plane. They sat back and watched until they had to react. After that, Nathan and I came immediately. Remember, we have the technology to travel great distances instantaneously," Emily explained.

"Did you know they were chasing me all over the country?" Franky asked.

"Not until tonight," she answered.

"What is this place, anyhow? I mean, it looks like a small city. Who lives here?" Franky asked gazing up some of the huge window-filled pillars.

"You'd have to asked your government that one," Emily said.

"The aliens bring good news," Nathan started, trying to change the subject. "The day in which an Earth Social Order enters a cycle that will bring them to a Collective Inception is coming soon!"

"When?" Franky asked still looking up at the massive pillars.

"The aliens say on December 23rd, in the year 2013!" Emily said excitedly.

"Twenty years!" Franky said smiling, "Square clouds, right?"

"Well, no. The process called Propitious Succession is going to start on that date. It may take a hundred years for a Collective Inception to occur. Only then will square clouds show up!" Nathan answered.

"Looks like they want all of us in the office," Emily said as one of the aliens stared out at them.

Emily, Nathan, Troy, Bob-O, Rebecca, and Franky stepped into the office. The alien looked at Franky, "You must make a deal," it said to him in his head.

Franky shook his head in acceptance. "Listen boy," the officer said. "We're going to let you go home. We're going to take care of that little mess back in Philly, and leave you alone. But, none of this ever happened! You understand?"

"Little mess!? You guys killed a human being! That's some little mess!" Franky said.

The alien looked at the officer. "Things got out of hand," the officer nervously explained to the alien.

Emily placed her hand on Franky's shoulder and whispered, "You still have to agree."

"Okay, I agree. None of this ever happened," Franky announced.

"Okay, good. What about the rest of you?" the officer asked. One by one they agreed to keep the events of the day, and all they knew about the alien mission, a secret.

"How are you going to clean up the mess in Philly? How am I suppose to explain running away to my family and employer?" Franky asked.

"How does written apologies from the US Government sound? We're going to say that two agents used excessive force in an attempt to apprehend what they thought was two murderers. The letter will say that those two agents were terminated, and that the actual murderer of the psychiatrist was apprehended and killed during a gun fight in Mexico. You just have to say that you two walked in on a murder, and then were chased by government agents who were shooting at you. You two panicked and hid out in a cabin in California for a few weeks, till the whole thing blew over. Hell, we'll even spring for your back pay," explained the officer.

"Did you know I was an abductee?" Troy asked his father.

"No! You were?" he said surprised as he looked over to one of the aliens.

"Yeah. I was. They trained mc to rebel against things that you stand for, like war. They trained me to give, not take. And I never knew why I was so different from everyone in the family," Troy said as a tear dripped onto his beard.

Colonel Bolger looked down to his feet, "I'm sorry Troy. I didn't know. You have to believe me."

"He didn't know," one of the aliens said to Troy non-verbally.

"If you come back home, I would pay for medical school?" his father asked as he fought to keep back tears of his own.

"I'd have to think about it," Troy answered.

"Okay, take as long as you want," said his father as he offered a handshake.

Troy stepped across the room and hugged his father. "I love you, dad," he said softly.

"I love you too, son."

"It's time to go," Franky said as he reached to hold Rebecca's hand. Rebecca, Troy, and Bob-O boarded the same ship. Franky paused before boarding and turned to give Emily a hug, "This good-bye stuff is getting old!" he said with a painful grin. "Can't you at least stop by for the holidays?"

Emily just smiled, and released him from her hug. "We'll see each other again," she said as she turned and began to walk toward her own ship.

"Wait!" Franky yelled. "Why didn't it work for me or Troy?"

Emily stopped and turned back around toward Franky, "Why didn't what work for you and Troy?"

"The lessons at Fathom Sound. Why didn't they work for us?"

"They did," she said assertively.

"Troy's living alone in a cabin, and I'm considering going into a lucrative buisness with my father-in-law," he replied.

Emily smiled, "If it wasn't for Fathom Sound Troy would today be a career soldier. And you? Well, I'm not sure where you'd be, but remember what you just did. You were willing to sacrifice yourself so that these military people wouldn't endanger your wife. That was pretty heroic what you did. You were willing to give the ultimate gift, your life! If that wasn't a test of your true character, what is?" she said as she stepped closer to him.

"Here," she said as she pulled something from her robe

pocket and handed to Franky what was in her fist.

Franky looked down into the palm of his hand and saw two seeds. "What? What is this?"

Emily smiled, but did not respond. She then turned back around and walked to one of the ships. Franky smiled as he suddenly realized what was in his hands. Emily gave him seeds of his favorite alien fruit, Salad Air Gate Fruit. He stared smiling, as she, Nathan, Troy's clone, and his own clone, boarded the silver vessel.

Franky stepped into the ship along with an alien, and met up with Rebecca. Slowly, the ship climbed up the tunnel leading back to the runway. After coming to a stop along side the Duchess and glider, they exited. Franky turned and hugged the alien, "You guys aren't so scary, " he admitted with a laugh, ". . .could use a little sun, but who couldn't?"

Franky departed the silver craft, and turned to take a final look inside. "Till next time!" he yelled.

And as he approached his wife and friends, they smiled, laughed and enjoyed the moment. "Man! What a ride it's been!"

Epilogue

Settling Down

"It was as true," said Mr. Barkus, *"as taxes is. And nothing is truer than them."*

-Charles Dickens

In the summer of 1992, Franky copyrighted his unusual theories surrounding Devout Reality. Of course, it wasn't until the following year when he first suspected he had been abducted by extraterrestrials as a child. After a few years following the December, 1993 agreement, he decided to tell of his journey through a fictional dramatization, thereby fulfilling his promise to Emily.

In 1995, Franky completed his novel and quickly signed a contract with a literary agent. Soon afterward, he agreed to terms on a publishing contract with a New York City publisher. The date for release was set for the Summer of 1997.

The summer came and went. Mysteriously, at the last moment, the publisher pulled out of the agreement. Both he and the agent were puzzled. After that, two additional publishing deals fell through under similar circumstances.

Franky worried that there were 'outside forces' at work, keeping the book from being published. When he spoke of the possibility that operatives from a black bag where causing the problem, Rebecca told him he was just being paranoid.

"Why would they bother?" she questioned. "There's no claim of truth to the account."

Yet, deal after deal dissolved.

He decided to terminate his agreement with his agent, and sought a publishing deal on his own. This was done in an effort to keep his contacts as low key, and quiet, as possible. He thought that if anyone was attempting to block his publishing efforts, he might succeed by proceeding in stealth. The strategy worked. Late in 1998, Franky found a small New York City publisher willing to print his novel.

Appendix

"With the advent of quantum mechanics, the clockwork world has become a cosmic lottery. Fundamental events, such as the decay of a radioactive atom, are held to be determined by chance, not law."

> *-Ian Stewart*
> *"Does God Play Dice?*
> *The Mathematics of Chaos."*

lbert Einstein resisted the idea of quantum mechanics til the day he died. In a letter to Max Born he writes, "You believe in a God who plays dice, and I in complete law and order." To him, the idea that the ultimate methodology in which our universe operates, its modus operandi, could not be ruled by chaos and disorder.

Einstein believed that there existed a much more far reaching theory that was yet to be discovered. This new theory would combine his classical view with quantum mechanics. In effect, to have it both ways. God plays dice, but in a manner that has rules.

Quantum mechanics, for those unfamiliar, is the study of wave-particle activity - subatomic science. The field is not easy to explain, and in fact, there are those who spend years studying the science, and are still confused. So, I can not possibly attempt to footnote the entire theory in an appendix. However, I think it is important to understand one aspect in relation to this book. One unexplained phenomena regarding quantum theory, is the fact that there seems to be interplay between the function of wave-particles and the observer measuring or studying the wave-particle. This suggests that consciousness affects reality. We've all heard the one that goes: "If a tree falls in the woods, and there is no one around to hear it fall, does it make a sound?" This is where that notion comes from.

In the book, Emily explains to Franky that the aliens live in harmony with the natural world. They do this as a collective whole. She says that each conscious being interacts with the subatomic particles around them. But because there is so much outside influence from other conscious beings, the particles become random. However, when all other conscious beings act in the same ordered manner, all particles in that same region, become ordered. Ergo: square clouds, symmetrical marching animals, etc. Nature becomes in harmony with the surrounding society.

The universe is ordered, as Einstein suggested. The universe is full of random occurrences, as Born thought. It is both. Currently, on planet Earth, it is random. But, if one day you are walking about doing whatever it is you do, and happen to see a strange looking cloud above with sharp edges, maybe it's even symmetric . . . smile . . . for we are one day closer. . .